All Alone in the Universe

By Lynne Rae Perkins

Illustrations by the author

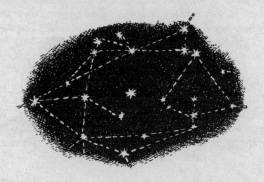

SCHOLASTIC INC.

New York Toronto London Auckland Sydney
Mexico City New Delhi Hong Kong

-It's for you, Mom-

ISBN 0-439-24323-8

12 11 10 9 8 7 6 5 4 3 2 1   0 1 2 3 4 5/0

Printed in the U.S.A.   40

First Scholastic printing, September 2000

Author photograph on back cover by Steve Davis

CONTENTS

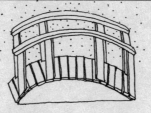

1. Where I Live   1

2. That Perfect Day in April, for Example   5

3. May   14

4. The Open House   26

5. June   34

6. At Some Point July Turned into August   48

7. September   73

8. October   90

9. The Hike   99

10. The Intruder   105

11. November   115

12. Thanksgiving Monday   122

13. Early December   127

14. Christmas Eve   131

Our town is called Seldem.

My dad likes to add, "If ever."

The bronze plaque in Memorial Park says that our town was founded by Lord Henry Seldem, from England, in 1846. No one knows who he was or why he came here. The next town west is Hesmont, also named after a lord. It's hard to imagine any lords living here now, though. The biggest house in town probably has four bedrooms. Maybe Lord Seldem's house was torn down when they put in the Seldem Plaza or the Thorofare. Or maybe he never lived here at all; maybe he just founded the town, and the next day he looked around and decided he'd be better off in Deer Church or River's Knob.

Memorial Park is a tiny green triangle on Pittsfield Street. Besides the bronze plaque, which is bolted onto an oily slab of coal from the Hesmont Mine, it has a flag-pole, a war monument, a bench you can sit on to wait for the bus, and enough grass for one dog to lie down on under the sign that says WELCOME TO SELDEM! A COMMU-NITY OF HOMES. When the dog stands up, it might want to trot two blocks south to the river and wash off because the grass (and everything else here) is coated with a light film of fly ash from the power plant in Birdvale, to the east. The dog would be kidding itself, though, because the river itself is fly ash (and who knows what else) mixed with water.

My dad says that we are descendants of Peter Stuy-vesant, who started New York City, and Lord Baltimore, who used to own Maryland. My mother doesn't believe this, but my dad says, "That and twenty-five cents will get you a cup of coffee." So we would seem to be up to our armpits in royalty and noble heritage, not to mention real estate. Nothing has made it all the way to 1969, though, except for some names. And names don't mean that much. If you think about them in a certain way, they can mean anything.

For example, my dad told me the other day that the stuff on the outside of our house is called Insul-Brick. It's supposed to look like bricks, but it's just a brick pattern, printed somehow onto thick sheets of a tar-papery, shingly-type material. No one would be fooled into thinking it's really bricks, but it looks all right. It keeps the rain out.

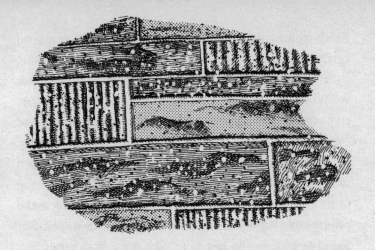

Now pretend you don't know that, and listen to the word: Insul-Brick. "Insulbrick." It sounds like a royal name, a name for a castle in Scotland or England.

I can picture it in gold, shining letters on a paperback book, with the gorgeous couple in flowing robes falling in love at sunset on horses in a garden with the castle, Insulbrick, in the background. . . .

Debbie of Insulbrick

Debbie of Insulbrick is not the gorgeous woman, though. Debbie is the girl up in the tower who has to finish ironing all the flowing robes before she can send carrier pigeon messages to her friends. That would be me.

In the first chapter, Debbie of Insulbrick's mother would be saying, "Why do *you* always send the first carrier pigeon message? Why doesn't Maureen ever send one to you, first? They have pigeons, too, don't they?"

Debbie would breathe an inward sigh of exasperation with her mother for expecting Maureen always to do the same things that ordinary people might do, like make phone calls. I mean, send carrier pigeon messages. But aloud Debbie would just say, "She does, sometimes."

Which I think was true, before last summer. Before last summer Maureen and I were best friends.

I know we were in May.

I'm positive we were, in April. At least I think we were. I don't know what happened exactly.

As people who get hit by trucks sometimes say, "I didn't see anything coming."

That perfect day in  for example

THE YARDS in Deer Church are so big that a better word for them might be *meadows* or maybe *parks*. They are perfect and beautiful and so big that you can have a picnic in one corner of the yard and the people in the house never even know you're there, because the house is so far away, and there are trees that block the view.

The only part of the house we could see from where we were sitting was the roof, with its dozens of peaks and chimneys poking up over the treetops like the skyline of a city. We were sitting on two park benches at the edge of a grove of birch trees, eating lunch out of our bike bags.

"See," Maureen said, pointing to the benches, "they *expect* people to come here."

"I wish they had put a pool in, though," I said. "I'm sweating to death."

"Cheapskates," said Maureen.

A few birds and crickets chirped, and some bees buzzed through the warm spring air. A car came and went somewhere, and there was the distant drone of one lawn mower. But there were no voices shouting, no screen doors banging. We could have been a million miles from Seldem. We chewed on our plain cheese sandwiches, made without mayonnaise so we wouldn't get food poisoning, and washed them down with warm, plasticky water from our water bottles.

"Let's ride back through Blentz," I said, "then stop at the Tastee-Freez."

"Okay," said Maureen, "but first, let's do our stomachs."

We plopped down on the silky, never-seen-by-its-owners grass and pulled up our T-shirts to expose our pale stomachs to the sun. Bathing suit season was right around the corner. We closed our eyes and drifted. The sun was warm. It had been a long ride, with a lot of hills.

"I wish I had a Coke," I said.

"Me, too," said Maureen.

"Do you have a suit yet?"

"No, do you?"

"No."

"No, me either."

There was a new kind of bathing suit I was thinking about, a two-piece. The top had two or three rows of ruffles in the front to "emphasize the bust." In my case

I was hoping it would make me seem to actually have a bust.

Joke: A flat-chested girl goes into a store to buy a bra. She opens her blouse and says to the clerk, "Do you have anything for this?" And the clerk says, "Clearasil."

Which pretty well describes my figure. And Maureen's.

The sun dazzled our eyes through our eyelids. Grass tickled the backs of our legs. In my daydream I was going to the pool in a ruffle-topped swimsuit, which was somehow also making my hair thicker and straighter, helping me tan without burning, and bringing me success in romance: there I was, talking and laughing with three of the twenty-seven boys I was currently willing to have a crush on but was unable to speak to. I wondered if I had asked them about their interests and hobbies. I strained to hear what I was saying in case it was something that could actually be said to a real person, but suddenly someone started shouting. My dream self looked around to see what this interruption in my perfect life was all about.

"Hey!"

The shout was coming from the outside, not the inside of my head. I rose, spinning, to the surface, and my dream self dissolved into a million rainbow-colored bits, like oil dissolved by detergent.

"You there!"

I lifted my head and saw a man walking briskly toward

us across the unknown wealthy person's emerald lawn. He was carrying something pointy that glinted in the sunlight.

Because I am the type of person who views being shouted at by people holding weapons as something to be avoided, I panicked. I grabbed Maureen's arm.

"Maureen!" I whispered. "We have to go. Now! *Wake up!*"

"I'm not asleep," she said. Rolling her head in my direction and opening one eye, she asked, "What? What did you say?"

"This is private property!" the man shouted across the fifty feet of lush green carpet that still separated us. The pointy, shiny thing he carried looked like a dagger. Or possibly hedge clippers.

"Oh," said Maureen. By the time she stood up, I was on my bike, poised to disappear from the neighborhood for several years or even forever.

"Maureen," I whispered more urgently, "let's go. *Now.*"

But Maureen just stood there. "Hi!" she called out. "What did you say?"

I couldn't believe it. From the sound of her voice, you would think an old friend had spotted us and was on his way over to say hello and invite us into the mansion for a lemonade. I turned to explain our situation to her. But then I thought I might wait a minute. Because when I saw Maureen's face, I knew that she had a different idea about what could happen next. Her idea was that it was going to be something good, something fun. This was basically always Maureen's idea. The amazing part was, just having the idea could make it be true. The trick was being able to think it. Maureen could think it almost anywhere.

I looked at the man with the hedge clippers to see what kind of idea *he* might have about what would be happening next. His tanned and wrinkled face was partly in the shadow of a cloth hat, but I could make out silvery eyebrows over crinkly, twinkling eyes. He had already decided we were not exactly a dangerous pair. He stopped about ten feet away and put  his hands on his hips. He was only pretending to be serious now.

"Now, tell me," he said. "Do you girls make a habit out of camping in other people's front yards?"

"Oh, come on," Maureen said. "This isn't someone's front yard! Where's the house?"

The hedge clipper guy glanced back over his shoulder at the miniature city beyond the small forest. "Right over there," he said.

"Oh," said Maureen. As if we didn't all know she knew that already, which I'm pretty sure we all did.

She studied the rooftops in the treetops. "It looks like

the house in *The Secret Garden*," she said. "Is there a secret garden?"

The hedge clipper guy seemed to be amused. He crinkled and twinkled a little more. "There's a garden," he said. "But it's no particular secret. Would you like to see it?"

"Yes!" said Maureen.

They both looked at me.

I was hesitating. I had one foot in the land of adventure, but my other foot was still on the pedal of escape.

The hedge clipper guy winked at me and said, "I'd say you were about to take off like a bat out of hell."

I got off my bike and leaned it against a tree.

He told us that his name was George and that he was the caretaker and gardener for the whole place, which even had its own name. It was called Webley. When we told him where we were from, he whistled and said, "Is that right? Seldem. That's a fur piece on a bicycle."

He led us through some dappled, leafy groves and a gate made of iron swirls into the garden. It was not like any garden I had ever seen. There were three parts, each part a few steps lower than the one before, until at the bottom you could lean against a stone wall and look out at the river. It was our river, but it looked better here. Serene and majestic. Maybe even clean. There were fountains and ponds. There were winding paths and statues. There were trees with branches that curved like snakes, trees growing flat up against a wall like candelabra, trees trimmed into the shapes of animals, and bushes growing in the shape of a maze.

"Wow," I said.

"No kidding," said Maureen.

"If I lived here, I would be in this garden all the time," I said.

"I'd enjoy the company," said George. He said it as if he meant it, and I thought about how every inch of the garden was made to be pleasant, to be pleasing, but no one besides us was there to be pleased. It could be lonely, I thought. Though as places for being lonely go, it wasn't the worst one you could pick.

"Of course there aren't any roses yet," George said. "If you were to come back in June or July, then there'd be something to see."

"Can we come back?" I asked.

"Sure," he said. "Just knock at the kitchen door over there and say you're here to see George."

"Okay," I said. I knew I would come there again. I felt it in my bones.

"I'll put you to work," said George.

"Okay," I said.

Back on our bikes, we rolled gently along the winding lanes of Deer Church. The road was so empty we could ride side by side most of the time. We peeked down the long driveways to catch glimpses of the houses.

"Let's stop there next time," Maureen said. She pointed to a house that looked a lot like the one where Snow White met the Seven Dwarfs, only bigger.

"We can't do that," I said. "George would be bummed if we stopped in someone else's yard." Maureen could sometimes forget about things like that.

"Oh, yeah," she said, "I guess you're right."

The houses started to shrink, and the yards, too, until they were shoeboxes set in the middle of postage stamps, and now we were in Blentz. We coasted down the main street of Blentz, then the main street of Hesmont, then the main street of Seldem. It's all one street, but each town has a different name for it. In Seldem it's Pittsfield Street, and that's where the Tastee-Freez is.

There was only one little thing that day that wasn't perfect. As I turned onto our street, I saw a moving van parked in front of the house where the Zolniaks had lived. A couple of men were trying to get a television set through the front door, and in the middle of the un-mowed lawn a woman was sunning herself on a chaise lounge. Her bright blue bathing-suit straps were undone, and she had yellow plastic eye protectors over her eyes.

I was just coasting by, minding my own business, when a chance gust of wind blew one of the big back doors of the moving van wide open, right into my path. I tried to swerve, but it was too late. I slammed right into it and was hurled in slow motion through the air. I was up there for so long that I had time to notice the sound of my bike, clattering down without me. I had time to look both ways and feel relieved that no cars were coming. Time to think, This is kind of interesting, and right now I'm still okay, but in a second I'm going to get hurt. Which I did. I met the pavement with great force and cried out, "*Aaaaagghhh!*" Or something like that. With a quickness that surprised me, I found myself jumping up and dusting myself off. I examined my hand and my leg, where gravel and flesh and blood were mingling freely. The lady in the chaise lounge lifted up her eye protectors and said, "You okay, hon?"

The hot, stinging pain brought tears to my eyes, but I said, "I'm okay. I'm almost home anyway."

"Okay," she said. "I'll take your word for it." And laid her head back down.

Other than that, though, it was a perfect day. Like every day with Maureen. They all were perfect.

CHAPTER THREE

On the morning of the first day Marie Prbyczka came to our school, the dawn's early light slipped softly into the bedroom where my sister, Chrisanne, and I lay sleeping. We floated through our sleep peacefully, like two pearls sinking through Prell, until the alarm clock ripped the quiet into two pieces, and the first piece fluttered out of sight forever. I pried one eye open so I could watch Chrisanne as she flung herself headfirst out over the foot of her bed and, tethered there by two fingertips, reached out with the fingertips of her other hand to plug in her electric curlers. Then she flopped back in a 180-degree arc onto her pillow and fell into solid, heavy sleep for ten more minutes. It was amazing and impressive. Especially since Chrisanne isn't very flexible. On most days she can hardly do a forward roll. It reminded me of dolphins leaping completely out of the water and flipping over in the air. You watch them and wonder, How is that even possible?

Our dog, Cupcake, curled more tightly into a doughnut-shape between my knees, hoping that if he kept his eyes squeezed shut, we would abandon our stupid idea of getting out of bed. Alas for Cupcake, it was a school day. He watched us reproachfully as we dressed, ate breakfast, and, one by one, left the house.

I walked to Maureen's house, where I sat in the kitchen and talked with Mrs. Berck, while Maureen mined the vast mountains of clothing piled around her room, looking for enough different items to dress herself completely. She never started until I got there. I didn't mind. I liked being in the Bercks' house. I liked the way everyone wandered in and out of the cluttered kitchen, picking up and leaving behind half-eaten pieces of cold toast. I liked how Mrs. Berck didn't seem to be concerned that there weren't any horizontal surfaces empty enough to sit down on. You got the idea that her mind was on more important things, like whether the cedar waxwings had returned. She kept binoculars and a bird book on the windowsill, and the tree in the backyard was hung with feeders.

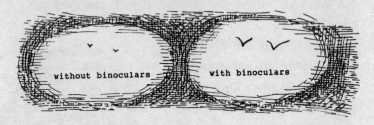

without binoculars   with binoculars

I found a small piece of empty wall I could lean on and watched Mrs. Berck sew a button on what was probably a garment since it seemed to have sleeves. She was standing up, too, in the middle of the room.

"Maybe we should join that religion where they don't use buttons," she said. "Since we can't seem to keep them on anyway." She broke the thread with her teeth and knotted it again for the next button. "Although," she went on, "holding your clothes on with straight pins sounds a little inconvenient, too."

By the time Maureen came downstairs with most of her clothes on, it was late. Really late. We pretty much had to run the whole way to school, taking brief pauses so that Maureen could swallow bites of toast without choking. We ran down Maureen's street, then down Prospect Hill Road, which is like running down the side of one of those Aztec/Incan/ Mayan step pyramids, but with trees and houses all over it. At the bottom there is traffic, so one has to stop, which if one is running, is done by grabbing hold of the street sign pole. Usually at this point one is hot, sweaty, and out of breath.

Maureen and I were. We had run down the hill, whooping and hollering like little kids, and we stood there, waiting for the light to change, breathing hard and laughing. Getting ready for the final sprint, Maureen looked up the street toward the school and said, "Who's that?"

I followed her squint. Marie and a guy were leaning against a car, passing a cigarette. I knew who she was. I had met her a few days earlier. She was the oldest daughter in the family whose moving van had knocked me off my bicycle.

"Her name's Marie," I said. "Her family just moved into the Zolniaks' house, on our street. But I thought she'd be at the high school." She seemed older.

We crossed the street, then stopped walking again. No one else was around. The late bell started to ring, and Marie's boyfriend drew her into an embrace. I guess you could call it a good-bye kiss. Well, some things are just too embarrassing to watch, especially first thing in the morning. Maureen and I turned toward each other.

"We're late," said Maureen, as if she had just realized that.

"I know," I said. "Let's go in the back door."

So we did. We had to climb a fence. It's not a high fence, and it's one of the ones that are made of a thick wire twisted together so there are footholds all over. Like this:

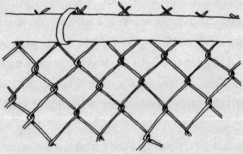

Usually easy to climb, but the tops can be tricky because sometimes the ends of the wire stick up above the top rail. As I make this drawing of the fence, I realize that it also looks a lot like the fishnet stockings I was wearing that day, which got caught on those wire ends sticking up. Suddenly there was a resistance to my descent and a burning pain as the wire ends dug deep gashes into the back of my thigh.

"*Aaaii*-eeee!" I yelled, clamping down in mid-yell since we were trying to sneak in late. Marie and her boyfriend looked over; the faint sound of their laughter rippled down the sidewalk. Maureen ran back and held my stuff while I unhooked myself and walked, half hopping, over the lumpy, battered roots and dried-up powdery dirt behind the school.

My bloody wounds seemed to be a good enough excuse for being late. Mrs. Radisz was too busy even to ask what happened. She just sent me to the nurse, who cleaned me up, checked my records for tetanus, and plastered greasy ointment, gauze, and adhesive tape in a large bundle around my leg. Fortunately, when I rolled my skirt down a couple of times, it covered up the whole mess. I threw the fishnets in my locker and wore my gym socks all day.

I don't know why I took those stockings home instead of throwing them away at school. I was taking them out of my purse when I heard my mother coming up the stairs. I didn't want her to know I'd been late for school again; it makes her crazy that I leave home so early and still get to school late. My mom tells a lot of madcap tales from her youth, but apparently she was always on time. Now she's a schoolteacher, so she's even more on time. I tossed the tights under my bed and dropped to my knees to hide my bare legs. I dumped my purse out onto the carpet and pretended to be sorting it out.

Mom peeped her head around the door frame. "How was your day, honey?" she asked.

"Fine, Mom," I said. "That Marie Prbyczka is in some of my classes at school. Study hall and gym." When you don't want someone to notice something, it's always a good idea to introduce a contrasting topic.

"Really?" she said. She was surprised. "Isn't she Chris-anne's age?"

"No," I said. "Fourteen. She flunked a grade."

My mother can raise her eyebrows one at a time. I wish I had inherited this, but I didn't. I also didn't get tongue curling.

"She seems pretty friendly," I said, "but I don't think we're very much alike."

"No," my mother said. "No, I don't imagine you are. Well, I suppose I'd better go start dinner. I need you to peel potatoes."

"Okay," I said. "I'll be right down."

As I was changing into my jeans, I thought about Marie for a minute. She was fourteen, but she looked older. Like thirty. She was the kind of girl the principal keeps changing the dress code for, but it won't make any difference unless he makes a rule that says, "No one may be Marie Prbyczka." I guess he could try, "You must open your eyes the whole way, walk like a nun, and look enthusiastic," but it would be hard to enforce.

I didn't think that Marie was beautiful, but I couldn't tell. She wore a thick layer of orangy-pink makeup that stopped suddenly at the edges of her face, making her neck and ears seem pale and dingy in comparison. Her long, heavy bangs were like window shades drawn down to let just a crack of daylight in. She wore beige lipstick that made her lips, which were thin anyway, practically disappear, except for the line where they came together. Her fingernails were long, chipped, and pearlescent. There was a bump on her nose.

I was surprised when she sat behind me in study hall that day and said my name. I was surprised that there was so much warmth in her voice. I turned around and saw sparks of life in her eyes. I liked her.

"Did you get hurt?" she asked. "We shouldn't of laughed, but you looked so funny."

"That's okay," I said. "I'm all right."

I liked her, but I held back, too. I don't know why.

I pulled on my sweatshirt and glanced in the mirror. I scanned my face to see if any interesting features had emerged. Michelle Patterson told me that it's a good thing I wear glasses because otherwise I'd be completely nondescript. That's the word she used. I think she was trying to make me see my glasses as a good thing, but I felt invisible for about a week and was surprised when people recognized me.

It's true that nothing about my face really stands out. My eyes have a regular eye shape. They're blue. I have a medium nose and medium lips. My teeth are straight, at least the ones that show. There is a mole on my right cheek and a dimple on my left cheek, but it's basically an average face. It's an okay face, but it wouldn't launch any ships.

Still, when I catch myself in the mirror sometimes, I think there is something there, some secret kind of beauty that flashes out if I'm laughing, or wearing someone else's clothing, or feeling messy and sloppy and wild. My mother doesn't see it that way, though, and most of the time she keeps me trimmed, combed, ironed, and tucked in.

My older sister, Chrisanne, has the kind of beauty that likes to be tidy. Her hair is blond, like mine, but thick and straight, and the barrettes and headbands are just for decoration, because her hair wouldn't dream of being out of place.

Maureen's beauty is more like mine, but her mother isn't as neat, as you already know. Maureen wears glasses, too, but she is farsighted, and they make her eyes look bigger and more beautiful.

For the next few days I wore long pants after school, even though it was warm. "I just feel a little chilly," I was planning to say if my mother asked why. She never did ask about that, but she did ask, as usual, why I was going to Maureen's house again.

"Why are you always running over there?" she asked. "Why can't she come over here?"

A million answers sprang to mind. It was more fun at Maureen's house, for one. It was less fun at our house, for another. However, the main part of my mind was still focused on my excuse for wearing long pants in seventy-five-degree weather, so all I said was, "Boy, I know it's nice out, but I still just feel a little chilly." I rubbed my hands up and down my arms and shivered, for emphasis.

Riding away from our less-fun house, I felt free and full of life. I coasted down Moyhend Street, bounced gracefully up over the curb onto the Bercks' sidewalk, and hopped off my bike. Mrs. Berck came to the door.

"Oh, hi, Debbie," she said. "Maureen isn't here. She took off somewhere with Glenna Flaiber."

"Oh," I said. "Okay. Bye-bye."

My balloon popped and shriveled and dropped to the ground with a quiet plop. I climbed back onto my bike and pedaled around for a while. I didn't feel like going home yet. Poor Maureen, though, stuck with Glenna for a whole evening. There was a low, ominous rumbling of thunder, and I headed back to my house.

"Why didn't they invite you?" my mother asked. I had wondered about that myself. But not for long. Missing an evening with Glenna Flaiber seemed more like good luck than a cause for regret. The storm exploded around us. The thunder was coming so quickly after the lightning we couldn't even count to see how far away it was. It was right there, the sound and the flash all at once.

Fresh spring breezes floated gently into the open bathroom window. The radio played the top ten countdown. Chrisanne, who takes voice lessons, was singing downstairs in her opera voice while she cleaned the living room. Mom was vacuuming in the bedrooms. I was scrubbing away at the bathtub when I heard the sweeper jam up and stop, and my mother's voice say, "What on earth?"

I heard her say this, realized that she was in my bedroom, and knew that I was going to have to explain something. I wondered what it was. I wondered if I was guilty or innocent.

Mom appeared in the doorway. In her hand were the shredded and bloodstained fishnet stockings.

"Oh," I said.

"'Oh'?" she repeated. "'*Oh*'?"

I told her about being late, about Marie and her boyfriend, about the fence. The color came back into her face.

"Why didn't you tell me? Why did you hide these under your bed?" she asked. Her voice was still upset, but softer.

"I didn't want you to know I was late again," I said. "I was going to throw them away, but I forgot."

"Show me your leg," she commanded.

I pulled down my jeans, and she looked at the three long, scabby scratches.

"It's not that big a deal," I said. "It's just a pair of tights. I'll pay for them with my allowance."

"It's not that," she said. "It's not that. I don't care about the tights."

She pulled me closer to her and said, "I was afraid that you had really been hurt."

I couldn't imagine what she was talking about, but I hugged her back anyway.

THE CORNER HOUSE

You could tell right away that the Prbyczkas were a little different from the other people living on our street. I mean, everybody is different, but the Prbyczkas were more different. They were different in different ways. Or it could be that they just didn't stick around long enough for us to get used to them. Maybe in a while they would have started to blend in. Maybe we all seemed that different at first.

If the rest of us were shrubs and neatly trimmed bushes, then Mr. and Mrs. Prbyczka were plastic potted palm trees, and their kids were wild, weedy brambles. Or maybe Mr. and Mrs. Prbyczka were like the big, shiny car parked in their driveway, and their kids were like the ragged blades of grass growing up through the cracks around it. (I guess in this case the rest of us would be, I don't know, mailboxes or something.) Because Mr. and

Mrs. Prbyczka, and their car, looked glamorous. Flashy. Mrs. P. was, we found out, a beautician, and her blond hair was teased and sprayed to look as if it were con-

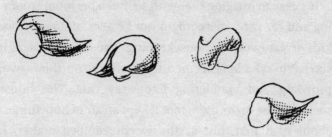

stantly blown by the Carefree Winds of Beauty. She wore unusual colors of lipstick, like Golden Plum or Iced Apricot, with matching nail polish. Her tight slacks often had glittering threads woven into the fabric. Mr. Prbyczka looked glamorous, too. He reminded me of Dean Martin on TV, with his handsome nose and thick, curly hair.

He wore his shirt with the top buttons open, and a gold

chain was there among his chest hairs, which were thick and curly, too. He didn't wear nail polish, but his nails were smooth, even, and shiny.

It's easy to imagine that with so much personal grooming and car care, there might not be a lot of time left for kids or yardwork or housekeeping. The seven (or was it six?) Prbyczka kids seemed to be always on their own, prowling and wandering like stray cats. The house seemed to be on its own, too. It kept an air of hopefulness about it at first, but as the weeds climbed higher, it quickly lost heart and started to shed chips of paint.

Toward the end of May, though, Mrs. Prbyczka called everyone on the street to announce that they were going to hold an open house. The next-door neighbors had probably been inside already, but no one at our end of the street had, and we all were curious.

"Are you taking something?" my mother asked our neighbor Fran. "A housewarming gift?"

"Yes," said Fran. "I think I am. I think I'll take a few jars of my spaghetti sauce. Maybe you could make one of your coffee cakes, with the nuts."

So, bearing gifts of food and goodwill, we traveled afar to the Prbyczkas' front door. Everyone seemed to arrive at once, and we all squeezed past Mrs. P. into the house. She was stunning in slim red pants and a fluffy tangerine sweater with the sleeves pushed up. You could tell she had no need for a ruffle-topped swimsuit. Her shoes were

those slip-on high heels that
I have never seen anyone
but Barbie dolls wear.

Her lips, fingernails, and toenails were all tangerine, and she was telling everyone to call her Babe. "That's what everyone calls me," she said, in her loud, raspy voice.

My mother and Fran nudged each other with their elbows.

"I'll bet," murmured my mom.

Fran choked back a laugh.

"You're so bad, Helen," she said.

The house no longer smelled of stuffed peppers and cabbage rolls, the way it had when the Zolniaks lived there. It looked different, too. Where there used to be a brown picture of Jesus knocking on a door and another picture of the Last Supper, now there was a bunch of golden grapes and a painting of a Spanish lady winking over a black fan with roses. Instead of rocking chairs layered in crocheted afghans, there was a red vinyl couch patched with bookbinding tape that didn't quite match and a cracked, white plastic, egg-shaped chair with a turquoise cushion. Everything was a little the worse for wear, but with six or seven kids, what do you expect? My favorite item was the black ceramic charging bull with a cigarette lighter in its mouth. The ashtray was a lime green blob of cooled molten glass, heaped with ashes like the leftovers of a Jell-O volcano.

As the living room filled up with people, I stopped noticing the interior decoration and positioned myself near one of the baskets of chips and pretzels that were placed here and there. After munching a few of these, and some mixed nuts, I looked around for Chrisanne. She was sitting on the stairs with our neighbor Tesey. Several steps higher was Marie. I gave a little wave and worked my way through the crowd to join her.

Marie looked bored. Or maybe her makeup was just so thick she couldn't move her face to show expression.

"Do you want some pop?" she asked.

"Okay," I said.

"It's in the kitchen," she said. "But it's probably easier to go outside." This wasn't exactly a joke, but there was something jokey in her voice. So I laughed.

In the kitchen the men were standing around holding bottles of beer and talking in hearty voices. Without really noticing us, they parted to make a path so we could get to the refrigerator.

We sat on the back stoop, watching the little Prbyczkas run in circles. The bigger ones were playing some kind of game where they piled on top of one another, then came crashing down, howling and yelping. Some of the neighbor kids were finding their way outside and joining in. It was turning into one big, noisy pile-a-thon, a football game without a football.

"It's getting pretty crazy out there," I said to Marie. I meant this in a positive way. Part of me was itching to get up and run around, too.

But Marie said, "Yeah, what a bunch of idiots," and I stayed sitting down. Not that I don't have a mind of my own, but I was trying to help her to feel welcome in the neighborhood, keep her company. A few minutes later a small Prbyczka was nearly creamed by a flying Szymanski, and I saw my chance.

"I better go make sure no one gets hurt," I said. "Wanna come?"

"What, are you nuts?" said Marie. Her voice indicated that she would rather drop dead. Still, she stood up and walked into the yard with me.

I organized a nice, safe game of slaughterhouse and soon had everyone running around in a less life-threatening way. Marie hopped gingerly around the edges, trying not to get involved any more than she had to. When the ball came to her, she batted at it with the palms of her hands. This accomplished nothing except the protection of her fingernails. I think she was enjoying herself in some way, though. As the game went on, she seemed to try a little harder, and she even laughed a couple of times. It was like water coming from a rock, which happened in the Bible, I think, but doesn't often happen nowadays. Then she realized what she was doing and slunk off around the house.

After everyone got "out" and started in on other games

in smaller groups, I decided to go back inside and see what was happening there. As the sound of kids faded behind me, I heard a car door shut and looked up to see Marie riding away in the old green car with her boyfriend. Don. Don, the sleazy. Yet he was also sort of handsome.

"A salesman?" asked my mother.

"Yes," said Fran. "For some company in Blentz—I forget what it is. He acts like a salesman, too. All phony jolly, 'isn't this terrific?' I felt like saying, 'Look, buddy, you don't have to try to sell *me* anything.' But you know how it is when you first meet people, Helen. It's hard to tell. They're probably very nice people. I shouldn't even say anything. They're certainly both very attractive."

"Yes, they are," said my mom. "The other day I drove by, and they were getting in the car, both dressed to kill. In the middle of the day. I don't know where you would go around here, even at night, dressed like that."

Fran laughed. "Well, Helen," she said, "I think maybe they go some places that you and I don't frequent."

"But what about the kids? I guess the oldest girl is old enough."

Fran laughed again. "Old enough for what? She doesn't look like she'd be too interested in baby-sitting." Her voice dropped, and I couldn't hear the next part.

Then my mother said, "Well, to each his own, I guess. I just feel for the kids. It's not their fault."

That night while I was talking to Maureen on the phone and poking around the crowded fridge for a snack, something popped into my mind, a piece of the day. It was a mental picture of getting pop from the Prbyczkas' refrigerator. Marie had opened the door and turned to ask me what kind I wanted. As she reached in to get it, something seemed odd. Now it came to me that besides the pop and the beer, there wasn't much of anything there. Some milk, I remembered seeing. And some ketchup.

"How about eggs?" Maureen suggested.

"Maybe," I said. "I don't really remember. But there wasn't much."

"Maybe they eat a lot of canned food," said Maureen.

"Maybe they eat out," I said.

"Maybe they're vampires," said Maureen, who watches *Dark Shadows* every day.

"I don't think so," I said. "They come out in the daytime."

CHAPTER FIVE

SUMMER RIPENED like a piece of fruit. But it was a piece of fruit with an unseen bruise, and it was ripening and spoiling at the same time. The bruise's name was Glenna.

The spoiling didn't happen overnight, but it didn't take long either, not as long as I would have thought or hoped. About as long as it takes for a moth to chew holes in your favorite sweater. A moth named Glenna. Glenna Flaiber.

Glenna had always been there. She went to school with us; her house was around the corner from Maureen's house. There was nothing especially wrong with her. There was nothing all that right with her either, not that I could see. To me, she was like one of those crumbs of wax that flake off the milk carton into your glass and you drink it anyway. It's too much trouble to fish it out, and it's not going to kill you.

Glenna was small and neat and ordinary and boring and irritating. That's what I thought. I thought Maureen felt sorry for her. The first time Glenna came along with us to the pool, I thought we were doing our good deed for the day. Then she came again, and I thought, Oh, great.

Pretty soon she was going everywhere with us, and I started to wonder how Maureen and I could get rid of her without hurting her feelings.

In the middle of June our family went on vacation.

"I'll miss you," Maureen said. "Send me postcards."

"Okay, I will," I said. "Have fun with Glenna." That was supposed to be a joke, but Maureen missed it.

She just said, "Okay. Call me when you get back."

the yard ornament was a silvery blue ball

We went to the ocean, to a cottage with white pebbles for a yard, on an island at the other end of twelve hours of driving. The last part of the road had ocean on both sides, then a drawbridge. When we opened the car doors and stepped out, the ocean breezes blew our sticky clothes loose from our sweaty skin, and for two whole weeks we forgot all about Seldem. I'd never asked myself before, I'd never had to, What if while we were off forgetting our regular life, what if our regular life, or some part of it, forgot about us? And then, what if it didn't ever remember?

If I thought about Glenna Flaiber at all, I guess I hoped that she would evaporate while I was gone. But she seemed to have congealed, like cold gravy and then cement, and I was the one turning into thin air.

There she was at Maureen's, the first day after our vacation. I walked over with a souvenir for Maureen, a pretty little round box with a lid, woven of straw. There were seashells around the edge, and colored straw flower patterns were embroidered on the top somehow. I had bought one for myself, too. They were cheap.

I found Maureen alone on the front stoop, with an Italian ice. "Maureen," I shouted, "we're back!"

"Deb!" she shouted back. "Hi!"

The screen door opened behind her, and Glenna stepped out. "Hi, Debbie," she said. She had an Italian ice, too.

"Oh," I said. "Hi, Glenna."

She smiled. It was the kind of smile where the parts of the face are in the correct position, but that's all you can say for it. She turned to Maureen and said, "Your mom is ready to go now." To me, she said, "We're going up to the carnival, in Birdvale."

"Wanna come?" Maureen asked.

"Is there room in the car, with your brother and sister?" Glenna asked Maureen.

"We can squish in," said Maureen.

"I didn't bring any money," I said.

"That's too bad," said Glenna. "Maybe another time."

"My mom can give you some," Maureen said. "Come on."

So we went.

It was weird.

The carnival in Birdvale is a little weird, even when you're happy. It's one of those fake fun places where the flashing lights and the music, the spinning rides, the booths full of prizes, and the smell of the food are all trying to convince you that you're having a great time. Personally I always have more fun when nobody's telling me I'm supposed to. I do like the rides, though. And the pizza. And I guess the lights and the music. And it's always fun to see who's there, especially who's there with who. Okay, it's fun. But slimy.

Slimy, because it's on the football field, which is down by the river and would rather be a swamp. The carnival people spread straw around, but it doesn't take long for all the polished toenails and white sandals to trample the straw into the mud, which then oozes up until everyone is dirty and wet up to the ankles. And slimy because of things like the prizes, which seem extravagant and luxurious while you're there, but if you ever win one and take it home, it turns out to be cheap and stupid.

Three is a lousy number in a lot of ways. One of those ways is that carnivals always have rides with seats that hold two people, so one person has to act as if she doesn't mind waiting by the fence or riding in a seat by herself or with some other leftover. This is why the Three Musketeers became friends with D'Artagnan. Not because of carnivals but because the number three is not a happy number. I know that in geometry the triangle is supposed to be an extremely stable shape, as in the pyramids, but in real life triangles are almost never equilateral. There are always two corners that are closer together, while the third is off a little ways by itself.

I was off a little ways eating some french fries from a paper boat, watching Glenna and Maureen ride the Calypso, when the idea first came to me that Maureen actually liked Glenna. Glenna was shouting over the noise and music of the ride. Whatever she shouted, it made Maureen laugh, and Glenna was laughing, too. They were spinning around together and laughing, their hands up in the air, slammed together by centrifugal force against the painted metal shell of their twirling car. I was in some other not-laughing universe, leaning on a fence that was standing perfectly still. The ride ended, and they tumbled and spun, still laughing, out of the car and through the gate. It seemed as if they might tumble right past me then, and

I blurted out, "Anyone want a french fry?"

Maureen spun my way and said, "Oh, yum!"

Glenna said, "No, thanks, I don't like greasy food."

This was wise, because I was planning to put a curse on her french fry that would make her throw up on the next ride.

"Oh, well." I shrugged. "More for us."

Then I said, "I love greasy food."

"Especially when it's salty," added Maureen.

We gobbled up the french fries, and now it was Maureen and I who were together while Glenna remained on her greaseless, unsalted planet.

"Let's go on the Zipper," I said to Maureen.

"Okay," she said.

So we did, and then we all played a game of tossing quarters onto plates balanced on bottle tops. I won a lime green cross-eyed bunny, which I gave to Maureen. I said, "Here, I want you to have this because you mean so much to me. And because I don't want to carry it around."

She grinned and said, "Oh, wow. Thanks a lot."

She glanced down at the bunny as she took it, then held it up to Glenna and said, "Does this remind you of anything?" Glenna crossed her eyes, they both laughed, and that was one for Glenna. Then it was her turn to ride with Maureen, and that was two. Glenna and I weren't taking any turns together, but no one mentioned that. Maureen was too busy having a great time to notice. Glenna was having a great time, too. I wasn't exactly having a great time. I felt off-balance, as if someone kept borrowing my right foot for a few minutes. As if someone were moving into my house while I still lived there.

The three of us wobbled around the dinky midway like a triangle trying to walk. I could see the grass already turning yellow under the parked trailers and their thick, tangled piles of extension cords. I could feel some odd new feelings—uneasy, spiteful, shapeless ones—creeping in.

I hate this stupid carnival, I thought, sitting on a bench across from the Ferris wheel as the other two points of the triangle rose up into the blue sky.

When we had spent all the money Mrs. Berck was willing to throw down the drain, we walked back to the car, where she was waiting, reading a book. It made sense geographically for me to be dropped off first. I got out and watched the car pull away. It was no different from a million times before. Through the rear window, beyond the collapsed Kleenex box and the green bunny, I saw Maureen's and Glenna's heads turn toward each other, and I felt myself falling away behind. But what could I do? I lived here; it was where I had to get out.

I walked over to rinse my feet off under the spigot. I didn't know how to wash away a crumminess that seemed to be swimming around in my heart. The garage door opened, and my dad pushed the lawn mower out from inside. He put a pretend surprised look on his face.

"Why, hello there, long-lost daughter," he said. "How's every little thing?"

"Okay," I said. I mustered up a smile from somewhere, mostly from his words and the sound of his voice. His words and his voice and my scrounged-up smile pushed the crummy feeling a little way off to the side, and I thought, Probably it was all in my mind.

It's because I was on vacation, I thought. I'm back now.

Don't be a dope, I thought. Maureen is your best friend.

But something was happening; something I couldn't see was shifting. When Maureen and I were together without Glenna, everything seemed fine. Almost. We had fun. We still laughed a lot. But before, when we laughed, we were just laughing. We couldn't help it; it just happened. Laughing and other kinds of thoughts or feelings traveled between us like breathing. Now I found myself holding on to good moments as if I could save them up and prove something to somebody.

It was getting hard even to *be* with Maureen without Glenna because Glenna was there so much. When I called Maureen on the phone, Glenna had already called. Or Maureen wasn't at home because she was sleeping over at Glenna's. Or I could hear Glenna's dippy voice in the background. Maureen always invited me to come along. And I would go, even though being together with Maureen *and* Glenna was not that much fun.

I couldn't figure out how Glenna managed to make so many plans so far ahead all the time.

On summer mornings, when you first wake up, you hear the birds chirping, and a shady green light filters through the leaves, and a coolness in the air means it still feels good to have at least a sheet pulled up over your shoulders. Maybe there is the faint whining and clanking of a garbage truck on a nearby street. For a minute or two you don't even think of any personal facts, like what your name is, or what town you live in, or what kind of life you might be having. Then you hear your mother outside talking to a neighbor or banging around in the kitchen, or you roll over and see your sister, still asleep in the other bed. You know who you are now, and your mind eventually gets around to what you might be doing that day. Which is when your heart feels light or sinks a little bit, depending.

From the backseat of the Flaibers' car, Glenna asked her mother what day they would be leaving for their vacation. My ears pricked up. An unexpected ray of hope lit up little dioramas in my head: happy pictures of a week (or two?) without Glenna. A scrap of song from a passing radio furled through the open window.

Finally, I thought. Finally.

Trying to keep my face calm, I waited for Mrs. Flaiber's answer.

"Saturday," she said. "But early. So probably Maureen should stay over Friday night."

What for? I thought giddily. So she can wave good-bye?

"That way she'll be sure to get up in time," Mrs. Flaiber went on. She threw a quick grin over her shoulder at Maureen. Maureen and Glenna grinned at each other. "We'll just roll you out of bed and into the car, Maureen!" said Mrs. Flaiber in a jolly way.

A tide of comprehension rushed in all around me, separating my little island from the shore where the three of them stood, getting into the car to drive away.

"Where are you going?" I couldn't help asking.

Apparently they could still hear my voice, although it sounded far away, even to me. At least Mrs. Flaiber could.

"Borth Lake!" she answered. "We have a camp up there! We decided to let Glenna take along a friend this year! We'll be sitting on each other's laps, but we figure, the more the merrier!"

I don't know what else she said, but all the sentences had exclamation points at the end. The water rose over my island and lapped around my ankles. I pressed my fingers into my knees, then lifted them and watched the yellow-white spots disappear. Maureen's knees were right next to mine. There was her hand on the car seat, with the fingernails bitten down below the nubs, as familiar to me as my own. I looked out the window at whatever was passing by. I felt mean and small, like something wadded up. Weightless, like something that doesn't even matter.

Mrs. Flaiber's voice chorbled merrily away, cramming the air with colorful pictures of capsizing rowboats and dinners of fish fried with their heads still on and the eyeballs looking right at you. I could hear Glenna telling Maureen that Borth Lake was the seventh largest man-made lake in the state.

"Really?" I heard myself say. "That is so interesting."

Suddenly it seemed to me that if I didn't get out of the car, I might completely disappear, and I said, "Mrs. Flaiber, can you let me off here?"

All three heads turned my way, and the abrupt quiet told me that I had probably interrupted someone.

"I just remembered," I said. "There's something I have to do. For my mom. I have to pick something up for her."

"Where do you need to go?" she asked. "We can take you there and wait while you run inside."

"No, no—that's okay," I said. "Actually I feel like walking."

"Are you sure?" she said, pulling adroitly over to the curb.

"Yep," I said. "Thanks. See you guys later. Have fun on your vacation."

Then, looking right into Maureen's eyes, I said, "Call me when you get back."

I tried to keep my voice steady, but my eyes were shooting out messages and questions and SOSs. I saw them reach her eyes and spark there in a flash of surprise.

She turned to Mrs. Flaiber and Glenna and said, "I'm going to get out here, too."

She was out of the car and closing the door before Glenna could follow. She leaned her head inside to say good-bye. Glenna and her mother wore the startled expression of fish twitching in the bottom of a rowboat or fried on plates. Mrs. Flaiber turned forward, and the car moved slowly back into traffic, crunching pebbles and grit musically beneath its tires.

I was surprised, too. A rush of exhilaration went through me. Maybe Maureen just hadn't seen what was happening, what Glenna was doing. Maybe I just needed to tell her. She dropped her beat-up tennis shoes onto the sidewalk and slid her toes inside.

"Are you mad?" she asked.

I just needed to explain it to her. Make her see. That was all. "Not mad," I said. Then I said it, what was in my heart:

"I just miss when we were friends."

I waited for her to get it.

"We're still friends," she said, standing on one foot to pull the back of her shoe up over her heel. She looked at me as if I had said something really humorous. "You goof," she said. "Hey, let's go down by the river."

She started off across the spongy, shimmering parking lot of the Seldem Plaza, leading the way through the canyons of wavy heat made by the parked cars. I followed her, like maybe I had my whole life. But wanting only to keep on doing that.

"You know what I mean," I said. A few shades less certain, though, that she would. "I miss the way we used to be friends. Before Glenna."

It crossed my mind that to anyone who happened to see us there, we would look the same as we always had. Debbie and Maureen. There they are. "Frick and Frack," my dad said. We would look the same. Did that mean something?

"You should give Glenna a chance," said Maureen. "She tries to be nice to you."

We moved through a short tent of shade next to the A&P and then the scrubby weeds that are the native flora of Seldem, the kind that can grow up through concrete as long as it's not the middle part that cars drive over all the time. The kinds of scratchy weeds that grow about ten inches high, then branch out and blossom forth in stiff, itchy exploded seedpods.

"Glenna doesn't want to be my friend," I said. "Glenna wants to be *your* friend. Glenna would be happy if I disappeared from the face of the earth in a puff of smoke."

We looked at each other. We both knew it was sort of true, and we smiled a little bit the way you can smile at something that is true when it is said out loud for the first time. It was a relief, in a way, to know that Maureen saw that part of it. For the moment that seemed enough. Going further seemed dangerous, like stepping off a cliff. Because I could also tell that Maureen wasn't going to be deciding right then and there to dump Glenna. She didn't see why she should.

I realize now that Maureen saw something in Glenna that I could not see. (I leave it to her biographers, or maybe to microbiologists, to discover what that is.) Not that I was trying too hard.

Anyhow, it felt safer then to leave that topic behind and take this bit of time with Maureen any way I could get it. To add it to the little pile of proofs that I hoped would add up to some charm that could eventually ward off Glenna.

So we squeezed between the dusty bushes to get to the riverbank, where we sank our feet into the silty mud, and sat on the low, bouncing branch of a big old tree that leaned out over the water. We crossed our legs like yogis and tried to balance there with our eyes closed. The shallow part of the river flowed along steadily, but in no hurry, about a foot below our branch, greenish brown, the color of a dollar bill. We opened our eyes and dangled our feet, making whirls and eddies form around them, talking about whatever, one thing or another. The sun must have been moving along up above the trees because the patches of sunlight shifted bit by bit over the moving surface of the water, lighting up patches of our shoulders and legs and the tops of our heads. In a way it was the best afternoon of the summer. But it was also like a prediction from the oracle at Delphi; it could mean practically anything.

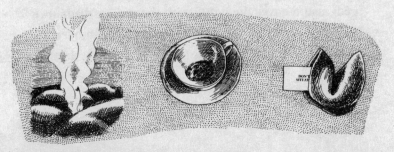

AT SOME POINT

W HILE MAUREEN and Glenna were away at Borth Lake,
I believed in the afternoon at the river. I believed it meant
something that Maureen had gotten out of the Flaibers'
car. She had promised she would call when she got back.
So I knew that she would. Maybe they had stayed a few
extra days. Then there would be unpacking. That takes
time. And probably the Bercks would be doing some
family-type activities. I knew she would call.

Here are some things you can do while you are waiting
for a phone call:

  1. Take a wine bottle that is empty. Mateus has
  the best shape. Or another kind of bottle, or a jar, if
  your parents don't ever drink wine. Which mine
  don't, but Fran gave me some bottles. You rip
  masking tape into a gezillion tiny pieces with ragged
  edges and cover the bottle with them. (See diagram.)
  Then, with a rag, you put brown shoe polish over
  the whole thing. Wipe most of it off. When it dries,

paint varnish on it. It will look old, like an antique.
You can use it for flowers
or as a candleholder.

Suitable for a gift!

2. Smash a windshield. *No, wait!* I don't mean like
a vandal! You will need parental assistance for this.
My aunt Alice told us how. You get the windshield
from a junkyard, and you paint one side of it with all
different colors. Let it dry. Wrap it in a large towel or
a blanket, and smash it to smithereens with a
sledgehammer. Probably your dad will have to do it.
The driveway is a good place. Then glue the pieces to
the outside of a big goblet from Jim's Bargain Store,
with the painted side in. Don't cut yourself! Put grout
(like in a bathroom) between the pieces and wipe the
surface of the glass bits clean. When the grout is dry,
paint it gold. Presto—another candleholder! When
you light the candle, it looks like stained glass. You
will have enough little pieces of colored glass to
make a dozen of these.

3. So, if you think you now have enough
candleholders, find an old wooden cigar box. Paint
it a nice color. On the lid glue a picture from a

magazine. Organically Grown clothing (with the beautiful woman and the deer) or Herbal Essence shampoo ads are good. ("Why do you want your hair to smell like grass?" my dad wants to know.) Varnish over it. Inside, on the bottom, glue a piece of felt. Call it a jewelry box.

You have now made fourteen Christmas presents, and it's only August. While you're in the Christmas spirit:

4. Blow up a balloon, and knot it. Wrap a ton of thread around it, and tape the end. Dip the whole thing in sugar water with starch in it, and let it dry. Then pop the balloon. The threads stiffen in the round shape, and they make good Christmas ornaments, especially if you hang them near a colored light; they have a glittery glow.

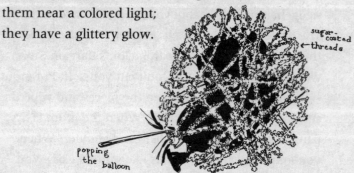

sugar-coated threads

popping the balloon

If you're lucky, a couple of days have gone by.

If you're not lucky, it's only time to watch *Hollywood Squares*.

*   *   *

Chrisanne and Tesey and a couple of their friends dragged me along with them up to the pool. They were funny and nice, and they acted as if they were so glad I was there.

Then Chrisanne suggested to my mom that the three of us go on a shopping trip downtown and maybe even have lunch in Horne's Tearoom. My mom said, "Sure."

So there we were, driving along and listening to the radio, when my mother decided, right out of nowhere, to pick up a hitchhiker. "Good Lord, look at that god-awful stringy hair," she said. Then she pulled over to the side of the road to pick him up.

She told Chrisanne to get in the backseat with me and invited him right into our car. He stooped over to look inside, with his sign that said DOWN TOWN and a wooden box, and asked, "You heading downtown?"

"Yes, we are," my mother said. "Where do you need to go?"

"Krepp Arcade," he said, "but anywhere downtown is fine." He climbed in.

"We're going right by there," said Mom. "We can take you to your doorstep."

You would have thought, the way they talked, that he was some long-lost friend. They talked about the weather, his shoeshine business in the Krepp Arcade, his family, how hard it was to get rides hitchhiking, where we all lived, and was he still in school (he wasn't).

Chrisanne and I were mystified. Neither of us remembered Mom ever picking up a hitchhiker before, and we wondered how she had decided on this one. He didn't seem like her type. Kind of grubby. On the shaggy side. He had bad grammar. And when he turned toward us, it was hard not to look at the purple blotches spread across his face like a map of islands. Chrisanne and I sat there in our dresses, hands in our laps. This guy was crudding up the niceness of our day. We were glad when he got out.

"Good luck!" my mother said. Chrisanne and I exchanged glances. We both were thinking, Good riddance.

"Thanks!" He smiled. His smile was friendly. We waved and smiled, too. Some of his presence seemed to linger behind in the front seat.

"I might as well stay back here till we park, Mom," Chrisanne said.

"He has a hard life," my mother said. "A hard life ahead of him."

"What happened to his face?" I asked her.

"A birthmark," she said, "like the one on your arm."

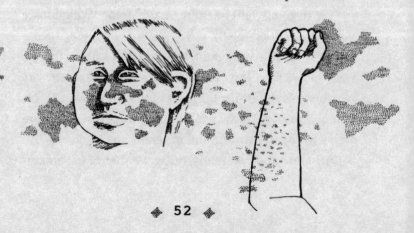

I turned my arm over and looked at the underside. My own blotches are small, calm, and inconspicuous at room temperature. When I am hot, they get reddish; when I am cold, they turn bluish purple. Most of the time I forget about them, until someone says, ''What is that on your arm?'' Sometimes they say it in a really rude way, as if it were leprosy or something, and I try to come up with some withering retort, but I usually can't.

''Oh,'' I said to my mom. Now I felt bad that I hadn't been friendlier. I was polite, but barely. I wanted another chance. ''He seemed nice,'' I said.

''Yes, he was a nice boy,'' said my mom. ''Though you'd never know it to look at him.''

Chrisanne wasn't paying attention to us. She had found a little runner in her nylons and was painting clear nail polish around it.

As we walked into Horne's, college girls in Bobbie Brooks outfits wanted to spray our wrists with perfume. The air itself seemed to be scented, and amid the polished old woodwork and the shining brass and the sparkling glass counters and chandeliers, the rich fabrics and the bustling escalators, remnants of the hitchhiker drifted lightly away. But later, when we waddled back to the car loaded up with paper shopping bags, his ghost seemed to be waiting there in the front seat. And even though he was gone the minute Chrisanne sat down, it started me thinking. Not so much about the hitchhiker as about my mother. Because usually I think I know what she thinks.

It's not hard to know; she expresses strong opinions in a forceful way on many subjects and after a while you can imagine what her opinion will be on a person or his/her actions. From committing crimes (which is definitely wrong) to choosing sandals with straps between the toes (not wrong exactly, but shows poor judgment). I would have thought that a high school dropout with greasy hair, hitchhiking, would be someone who had made at least three bad decisions and would have to face the consequences without any help from us. Yet sometimes she reaches out with warmth and kindness to the most unlikely people. Without making a big deal about it, as if anyone with half a brain would have done the same thing. I keep trying to figure out how she chooses.

What was it, for example, about the hitchhiker?

I think that in a way my mother is like a proper, immaculately kept house with a secret mark made on the fence by hoboes, to tell other hoboes that a woman lives here who will feed you. If you work. And some people can look at my mother's composed face and see the secret signs of welcome.

Bobby Prbyczka could see them. He had been coming to our house in the morning since June, to have coffee with my mother. I guess he saw her sitting there one day, in her lawn chair on the front porch, and invited himself on up.

"Any coffee left in that pot, Mrs. Pelbry?" he said.

She filled a green mug with milk and splashed some coffee in, for color. After that he came almost every day.

Mom liked it that he came, in the way that people like it when dogs or cats come right up and nuzzle them and want to be petted. She also liked it in the way that first-grade teachers, one of which she is, like six-year-olds, which Bobby was. But mostly she liked it just because Bobby was Bobby, a skinny little boy with shiny, happy blue eyes. Bobby's scrawny legs dangled out of hugely wide, but very short, shorts, and a small shirt stretched around his small chest. His hair was colorless like sand, but in the morning sun each tiny crew-cut hair glowed golden white, his happy eyes sparkled blue, and he was brown with summer. He spoke in an unexpected voice, booming and hoarse, saying words that were unexpectedly polite and grown-up–sounding.

"Looks like another hot one, don't it, Mrs. Pelbry?" he would say.

Or, "I see you're painting your gutters. That's a very attractive color."

Or, "Did you'ns see the fireworks up at Birdvale last night? Spectacular. Just spectacular."

"He cracks me up," my mom would say after he left, but while he was there, she was serious and attentive. Their conversations floated up through my window as I lay in bed, waking up, and I listened. I couldn't really help it.

"How are Mr. Pelbry and the girls?" Bobby started off one morning, as usual.

"They're fine, thank you," my mother answered. "And how is everyone in your family?"

"Fine," said Bobby. "Just fine."

He paused.

"Well, my brother Jerome, he ain't fine. He's got poison ivy all over his whole body. Even including his eyelids. They're swelled shut."

"Oh, dear," said my mom. "Where did he get it?"

"Down the woods, I guess," said Bobby. "He don't know what poison ivy looks like. I know what it looks like; it has three leaves."

"Leaves of three, let it be," said my mom.

Bobby laughed. "You must know a lot of poems from being a teacher," he said.

"And then my one other brother, Anthony," he went on, "he was riding his bike yesterday, and he rode off the edge of a loading dock over at that old factory building in Hesmont. He landed on his head and had to get eighteen stitches."

"Oh, gracious!" said my mom. "Your poor mother!"

"My brother's the one who had to get the stitches," Bobby pointed out. "He looks like Frankenstein. But he looks better than Jerome. Jerome looks like the Blob. Anyways, we all got to ride to the hospital in my sister's boyfriend's car because my mom and my dad was both at work, and my sister's boyfriend drives really fast, like a race car driver. And my mom had to meet us there, and she had to leave some lady's head in the sink and borrow someone else's car, so she was yelling at Marie for not watching Anthony. But Marie can't help it if Anthony don't look where he's going.

"So then Eileen and James started bawling right in the emergency room. Which turned out really good, because my mom said if we would all just shut up, we could get ice cream after. So everyone did, except for when Anthony got his stitches, and my mom said that don't count because anyone would yell who was getting their head sewed up. I even got the kind dipped in chocolate.

"It was a tremendous day," he said. "Absolutely tremendous. Except," he added, "that my mom and dad had a fight since we got home late and there wasn't time to cook any dinner. My mom put a bunch of those Tater Tots in the oven, but my dad said that wasn't dinner and he was going down Crystal Bar for a steak sandwich. My mom was steaming. She said, Why didn't he get a room there, too?

"But when my dad come home, him and me listened to the ball game on the radio. Did you hear that game? Did you hear that catch by Roberto Clemente?"

"Yes, I did," said my mother. "The one where he practically climbed the wall and reached way up with one hand?"

Bobby pressed up to the screen door

"That's the one," said Bobby. "Amazing."

Glancing out of the car window, I saw that we were getting close to home. My thoughts rose from the depths of my mother's relationships with Bobby and unknown hitchhikers up to the shallows of what was inside all the shopping bags that surrounded me on the backseat. I poked through a few of them, looking for my new hair holder. It was the kind Wilma Flintstone might use. I found it at the bottom of a bag, wrapped in tissue. I pulled my hair back to try it out and accidentally glanced out of the car window.

"Isn't that Maureen?" asked my mom.

"Uh-huh," I said.

"I thought she was on vacation," said my mom.

"She must be back now," I said.

"Do you want me to let you off here?" asked Mom.

"No, that's okay," I said. "I'm kind of tired. I'll just go home."

"Was that Glenna Flaiber with her?" asked my mom.

"Yeah," I said.

"She's starting to look so much like her mother," said my mom.

"Yeah, she is," I said.

On the fifth or sixth afternoon in a row that I had walked next door to sit with Fran in her carport and suck on lime Popsicles, she asked me, out of the blue, what I was waiting for.

"Hmm?" I said.

"What are you waiting for?" she repeated.

I tried to think whether something was supposed to happen that day, but I didn't think so. "I'm not waiting for anything," I said. "Why?"

Fran nipped a little chunk from her Popsicle and held it in her mouth as it melted. She folded her arms and looked at me. "You've been over here every day this week," she said. "Now, you know I love you dearly, and I'm always glad to see you, but this is not like you. You're young. It's summertime. You're supposed to be out running around with your friends. What's going on?"

Oh, I thought. That.

I didn't want to talk about it. I looked out at the street where a couple of Prbyczka kids were drifting by like tumbleweeds. Some drops of rain sent them skittering off toward home, then the clanging of the Goodie-Bar truck brought them closer again, digging in their pockets for nickels and dimes.

"It's starting to rain," I said. Brown, wet circles the size of pennies were appearing on the concrete beyond the carport. A few, then dozens, then hundreds, and then the raindrops searched in vain for a dry place to moisten. They just had to fall anonymously into the wetness. It was a summer rain, as warm as bathwater. We sat there watching it come down, listening to the drumming on the roof and the dripping from the gutter.

"You know," said Fran, "your life isn't going to start when this thing happens or when that person calls. Your life is happening right now. Don't wait for someone else to make it happen. You have to make it happen."

"I know," I said, even though I didn't know that. I didn't know it at all, and I didn't want to know it either.

So I just said, "I know."

And then I said, "I will."

"There are plenty of fish in the sea," said Fran.

"I know," I said again.

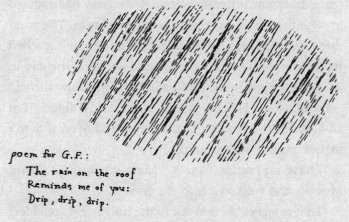

poem for G.F.:
The rain on the roof
Reminds me of you:
Drip, drip, drip.

Maureen didn't call. Day after day she didn't call. I ran out of good excuses for her not to call, and other kinds of reasons started seeping into my head and filling it with sludge. I could have called her. I kept thinking I would, in a day or two. I mean, What difference did it make, really, who called who?

One day I told my mom I was going bike riding with someone from school. I told her that we were taking lunches and riding out to River's Knob. She seemed happy that I was doing something with someone. But I wasn't doing something with someone. I was going by myself. I started out just gliding along as if I didn't have a plan. But I think I knew all along that I was going to George's garden.

When I realized that I was going there, I thought it was

because I felt so alone and I wanted to be in that beautiful, lonely place. The hot, gritty wind filled my eyes with tears, and some other tears from deep in my heart mixed in with them and streamed down my cheeks. The wind dried them all and left a stinging film. When I reached the corner with the birch trees and benches, the day in April came back to me and a thickness filled my throat.

I'm all alone, I said to myself. Then I said it aloud. "I'm all alone in the world." I said it over and over. It didn't matter; no one was around.

"I have no friends," I said. "None. Not any." I got off my bike and walked it into the grove.

"I am *so alone!*" I cried out to the universe. I could feel my face crumpling up. The garden was too far away. I sat down on a bench as the warm tears gathered behind my clenched eyelids.

"Well, not completely alone," said a voice. "But if you prefer, I can go away. This trimming will keep."

I looked around. It was George. I tried to smooth out my face.

"Hi, sunshine," he said.

"George," I said. "Hi." I searched for words. "How are you?"

"Happy as if I knew what I was doing," he said. "If you came to see the roses, they're a little past their prime, but they're still blooming. Everything else is growing like weeds. Including the weeds." He paused, then added, "That is, unless you're in a hurry."

"No, no," I said. "That's why I came. To see the garden, I mean."

"Well, come on then," said George.

I leaned my bike against a tree, and George handed me a pair of shears to carry. I wondered if he had noticed my reddened, watery eyes. I pulled out a Kleenex and said, "My allergies are driving me nuts."

"That time of year," said George. He pulled out a bandanna and blew his nose, too.

We walked through the cool, shady grove and into the rich person's garden. I had to catch my breath. I remembered the garden as elegant and calm, but summer had flipped a switch, and now it was a crazy explosion of color, a puzzle of light and shadow, full of spicy fragrances and the sun-warmed smells of dirt and stone and things growing. I stood still and looked around, trying to make sense of it all.

Some of the trees were heavy with fruit. The ponds were alive with goldfish. Flowers were everywhere. As my eyes sorted it out, I realized that a person was there, too, sitting at a table under an umbrella. Maybe the rich person herself, in madras plaid shorts and a sleeveless denim blouse. Her thick silvery hair was chopped short and tucked behind her ears. She looked up from her newspaper.

"Who's your friend, George?" she asked pleasantly. Her voice was warm and calm and clear.

"This is my assistant," said George. "Linda."

"Debbie," I said.

"Excuse me," said George. "Debbie. She's come to help me catch up on some trimming. Debbie, this is Mrs. Brown."

Mrs. Brown rose halfway and held out her hand. I went over and shook it.

"Nice to meet you, Debbie," she said. "Please, call me Martha." She turned to George. "George, do you and your assistant have a few minutes to spare for blueberries? I was just about to have some, and I'd love the company."

"I imagine we can spare a few minutes from our labors," said George. "Rest our weary bones."

"Good," said Mrs. Brown. And off she whisked, down a winding brick path toward the big house.

"I guess we'd better have a seat," George said to me. "The boss wants us to eat some blueberries." We sat down on striped cushions tied to curved chairs of iron mesh. The tabletop was ripply glass, like a thin slice of ocean. I moved my hand down and up underneath it, watching it get blurry and then clearer.

"So, where's your partner in crime?" said George. "What was her name?"

"Maureen," I said.

"That's it," said George. "Maureen. She wasn't up for a marathon bike ride this time?"

"Nope," I said. But just saying nope didn't seem like very polite conversation, so I added, "Maureen has this other friend now. She's probably doing something with her."

"I see," said George. "A previous engagement."

"I guess so," I said.

"Too bad," said George. "She's missing the roses. Maybe next time."

"Maybe," I said. "But probably not. She does things with this other friend practically all the time now. So I—" I stopped.

"I—" I tried again. "I'm—" The tears were right there, ready to pour out if I said another word.

"You're all alone in the universe?" George suggested helpfully.

His voice was gentle and kind, and when I looked at him, his face was solemn. So the only way I can explain what happened next, which is that we both burst out laughing, is that sometimes laughing and crying are almost the same thing. They're not all that far apart sometimes. I was laughing and crying both, and then I started to hiccup, too.

As I was trying to catch my breath, I said, "I came here to cry in the roses."

"Looks like you got what you came for," said George. "One way or t'other."

"What's everyone laughing about?" asked Mrs. Martha Brown, who was back with a tray full of napkins, sparkling silver, frosted glasses of iced tea, and delicate china.

"Debbie is alone in the universe," said George.

Mrs. Brown smiled. "That always makes me laugh, too," she said. She set the tray on a low wall nearby and gracefully moved its contents onto the shady glass table-top. After sitting down, she sprinkled powdered sugar over her blueberries, then poured thick cream on top. She put a spoonful in her mouth. She closed her eyes for a moment and shook her head slowly.

"Magnificent," she pronounced. "The most magnificent blueberries I have ever tasted. Tell me what you think."

She sat waiting for us to try them. The mountains of blueberries waited, too, dusky, round, and bluish purple in the porcelain bowls. Why did they look so odd? Then I knew.

"Are these raw?" I asked.

Mrs. Brown lowered her spoon. "Fresh," she corrected me. She looked at me curiously and said, "Don't tell me you've never had fresh blueberries."

"I don't think I have," I said. "Only in pie. And pan-cakes."

"You don't say," she said in wonderment. "Well, here." She reached over and sprinkled my blueberries with the sugar and poured the cream over them. "Try that," she said.

"I don't think I've ever had real cream before either," I said.

She looked over at George and said, "This country really is falling to pieces, isn't it?"

"In a handbasket," he said.

"I've had iced tea," I said.

Mrs. Brown chuckled. "All is not lost then," she said.

I tried a spoonful of the raw fruit and milk. It seemed like a weird idea, but it would have been bad manners to refuse.

The taste was incredible. I closed my eyes for a moment. I shook my head slowly and said, "Magnificent." I wasn't trying to copy Mrs. Brown; it was just all there was to say. Suddenly I wondered if the huge bowl of berries would be enough. Then I wondered if everything rich people had was better than what regular people had.

"Are blueberries expensive?" I asked.

"A little," answered Mrs. Brown. "But I think an occasional bowl of blueberries is within the reach of most people. A small compensation for being alone in the universe. Which, by the way, you aren't, you know."

"I know," I said.

"I'm here," said George. "At least I think I am. Though sometimes it's open to question."

Mrs. Brown's smile held traces of pink lipstick. There was a sort of light blond peach fuzz on her tanned face, and her blue eyes were calm and thoughtful when she turned them my way.

"But tell me, Debbie," she said, "what is it that's making you feel so lonely today? Can you tell us?"

I hesitated. What was I even doing here? I didn't know these people. But I hadn't been able to talk about it with anyone I did know. A few yards away a squirrel had found a piece of frayed rope. He had dragged it in his teeth to the trunk of a tree, and now he was trying to climb up with it. We all watched him while I tried to think how to answer. There were some things I didn't want to say out loud because if I did, it might mean they were true.

The squirrel kept dropping the rope. Each time he scurried down and tried again. Some time had passed now, and I thought I should say something. My throat hurt, and I felt I had to say it fast.

So I told them about how the person who had been my best friend since the third grade was spending all her time with this other person now. I might have said some unkind words about the other person.

"I can't believe it," I said. "I'm just left by myself, like we were never friends, like I don't even exist." I didn't understand, I said, how someone could just forget about a person.

It was more than I meant to say.

The rope fell to the ground again.

"George, help that poor squirrel, will you?" said Mrs. Brown.

George lifted the rope and draped it over the branch. The squirrel fled, then cautiously returned and scrambled up the tree. I wondered if they had even heard me. I was wondering why I had bared my soul to total strangers when Mrs. Brown nodded her head thoughtfully.

"I had a husband who did the same thing," she said to

me. "I got a house out of the deal," she added, nodding in the direction of the house, "but all in all, I would have preferred the husband. It's very painful, isn't it?"

I nodded. George was nodding, too. We were like a field of tulips in a breeze.

"And hard to let go," she went on. "There's no getting around that. But you must remember, even if you never understand what happened, what went wrong, that you will have friendship again, good friendship. Because you are a person capable of friendship. And sooner or later there will be someone who deserves you."

"There's nobody like Maureen," I said.

"No, of course not," she replied. "Apples and oranges. In the meantime, we can eat these nice berries and enjoy one another's company. Wouldn't you say so, George?"

"By all means," said George. "With a few moments set aside here and there for earning a living. Which I had better get back to directly before the weeds grow right over us."

"Yes," said Mrs. Brown. "I have some things to do, too. But make sure Debbie sees the lower garden. Especially the path to the river. That's my favorite."

To me, she said, "It was lovely to meet you, dear. Please come back."

And off she whisked again, down the red brick path. Like a fairy godmother. Mine maybe.

It was late in August, when we were tired of watching reruns, that my dad and I tuned in a dance performance

on Channel 13. Mom and
Chrisanne would have flipped
right past, but Dad and I
like to watch cultural programs
now and then. We had a TV tray with chip dip and pop.

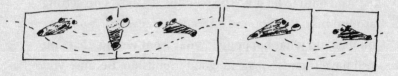

Cupcake's alert gaze followed each chip that left the bowl.

The dancers were spinning around in a big group, and
then two of them, a man and a woman, were in the spot-
light as they climbed up onto a sort of pedestal. They
were in love. The man lifted the woman into the air and
held her there with one hand. She arched her back and
her knees were bent so that her toes pointed up.

"How come you never lift me up that way?" joked my mother, who had come into the room to empty the wastebasket.

"Call the ambulance," said my dad. "I'll give it a try."

The man and the woman had been dancing for quite a while when suddenly another woman was on the pedestal with them. You could tell there was not room for three people to fit up there, although they did some amazing contortions trying.

"I think one of them's going to fall off," said my dad.

"I hope it's the new one," I said. "She's butting in."

But it wasn't. The man started twirling with the new one, and when the first woman tried to pry them apart, the man gave her a little push, and off she flew. He acted as if it were an accident, but I could tell it was on purpose.

"That wasn't very nice," said my dad.

She landed in a graceful heap and sat there looking gracefully back at her lost love and his new flame as they flounced around.

She was so bummed. She felt so alone. Slowly, so slowly I didn't notice it at first, the circle of light that she was sitting in widened, and there were all those other dancers, still dancing around. (Probably they had stopped while they were in the dark.) A few of them spotted her and tried to get her to join them. She didn't want to, but finally she did in a halfhearted way just so they'd stop pestering her. Bit by bit she started to be happy again.

The two on the pedestal were having an argument now.

"Serves them right," I said. But the one who had been dumped didn't even notice. She was having too much fun.

Sometimes you see something at just the right time. On another day I might have looked at those dancers and noticed what good shape they were in and wondered how they kept their costumes on. But this time, as I sat there, I thought I knew just how she felt, the one who had fallen from the pedestal. My dance on the pedestal was my friendship with Maureen. I still wasn't sure how I had lost my balance and fallen off. Or whether I was pushed. Everyone around me was trying to get me to dance again. The thing was, I hadn't quite given up on getting back up there. I still believed it was the only place where I could be happy.

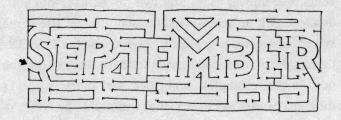

I HAD this idea that in September Maureen and I would walk to school together the way we always had and the awfulness of the summer would just end. Two days before school started, I braced myself and called her on the phone.

"Sure," she said. "Where have you been? Did you go on another vacation?"

"No," I said. "I've been around. Just hanging out, I guess." I tried to say it lightly. As if I hadn't been left behind and forgotten. A grain of sand at the beach. A footprint on dry cement.

"See you Tuesday then," I said, all carefree and cheery.

"Great!" said Maureen.

It sounded pretty good. It felt like old times. Maybe I really had imagined things. I could probably get used to Glenna. Maybe I could even learn to like her. Stranger things have happened. Astronauts have walked on the moon.

Three wasn't such a bad number. It had to be better than one. Even the Three (three!) Dog Night song, "One is the Loneliest Number," says that two can be bad, too, but I don't think it mentions anything about three. The Three Wise Men seemed to get along all right. Also the Three Little Pigs; Peter, Paul and Mary; the Three Stooges (maybe not the best example); Tom, Dick, and Harry, whoever they are. I would give it a try. How bad could it be?

So off we went, the three of us together, heading down Prospect Hill Road, side by side by side. Maureen was in the middle. It was a tight squeeze on the narrow sidewalk. Every few yards, roots from the sycamore trees had lifted up chunks of the concrete, and only two people could pass. Glenna and I both maneuvered ourselves to try to make sure it was the other one who had to go ahead or behind for a couple of seconds, all the while chatting in an offhand way about this and that. Then, just when I thought I was doing okay, Glenna looked back over her shoulder at Maureen and said, "I wonder if we'll see the Event today." Maureen laughed.

"What event?" I asked.

"Oh, nothing," said Glenna. To Maureen, she said, "I saw Handsome Walker and Lips at Tastee-Freez yesterday."

"Were they holding hands?" asked Maureen.

"They had their arms around each other's waists," said Glenna. "The Nose was there, too, and you should have seen him giving them the hairy eyeball."

"The Nose?" I asked. "What are you guys talking about?"

"I can't tell you," said Glenna. "It's a secret."

I turned to Maureen. "Can you tell me?" I asked.

"If I told you, it wouldn't be a secret," she said.

"But I'm your friend, too!" I blurted out.

"I promised I wouldn't tell anyone," she said.

Glenna smiled sweetly.

"Maureen!" I pleaded.

"Maybe you could guess," she said. "And I could nod my head if you guessed right."

So that's what we did for the next three or four days. Maureen and Glenna had spent the last month making up a secret code to talk about people and their girlfriends and boyfriends. It was stupid. I was desperate to know it anyway.

I started to bring up topics that would leave Glenna out. I told Maureen about going back to George's garden, though I didn't mention why I had gone there. I talked about chorus, which Glenna wasn't in, and gym, which she wasn't very good at. Glenna came up with new secret words I had to guess and made plans with Maureen that, for all sorts of reasons, couldn't include me. I brought up things Maureen and I had done together over the years. Glenna had fresh things.

It was junky. Maureen didn't see why we couldn't all just be friends. I would have thought that, too, if I were the one everyone liked.

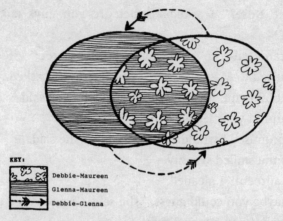

KEY:

Debbie-Maureen
Glenna-Maureen
Debbie-Glenna

On a morning that seemed at first like all the others, I walked to the corner of Maureen's street. My feet paused as I looked up toward her house. Then, to my surprise, my feet started up again and headed down Prospect Hill Road. What am I doing? I wondered. The rest of me wasn't feeling nearly as independent and free-spirited as my feet seemed to. They stepped forward in a determined way, and the rest of me, since it was attached, couldn't help going along.

From Moyhend Street down to Birch, my feet trotted past the new brick houses and the cinder alley, then the older houses with porches and front yards that are lower than the sidewalk.

From Birch Street down to Lillian. Small clumps of kids

drifted from their houses and the side streets onto the broken sidewalks. My feet, still moving briskly, stepped out onto the bare roots and dirt between the trees to go around them.

From Lillian Street down to Pine. Ahead of the crowd now, I let gravity pull me down to the bottom of the hill. Only a few kids were sitting on the steps and benches outside the school. I walked past them, pulled open the heavy door, and went inside.

Now, what? I thought.

"Where were you this morning?" It was Maureen, accompanied by her faithful leech, Glenna. I looked up from where I was squatting, searching for change in the bottom of my locker. My Maureen. Not my Maureen. But Maureen still. At least this time she had noticed I wasn't there.

That's something, I thought.

That's not enough, said a voice inside me.

It's all I have, I thought back.

You will have friendship again, said a third voice. Good friendship. Who said that? I wondered.

"I had to come early," I said aloud, "so I could go to the library and finish my civics paper." I had never lied to Maureen before. I waited for her to see through my flimsy alibi.

"Oh," she said, believing me. How could she believe me? Something inside me was jumping up and down,

waving its arms, and yelling, "It's not true, it's not true!"
I looked back into my locker so she wouldn't see it.
Locker doors were banging all around.

"Let's go," she said.

"We're going to be late," whinnied Glenna.

"You guys go ahead," I said. "I'll catch up in a minute."

I kept moving things around in the bottom of my
locker. Then I stood up and moved things around in the
top of my locker. A large lump was in my throat, and I
hoped I wouldn't have to speak to anyone. The din of
the hallway quieted behind me. Classroom doors clicked
shut, sealing in the clatter and the racket, putting the lids
on jars filled with bees.

I was still standing there in front of my locker. I
couldn't seem to move. I studied the pictures taped inside. There was a mirror taped inside, too, and I looked
into it. I tucked my hair behind my ears and put on some
lip gloss. Since I still seemed to have the use of my arms,
I crossed them in front of me to hold myself together. It
was starting to look as if I might stand there all day when
I heard footsteps approaching, footsteps with authority.
I thought I should act busy, but my locker was in perfect
order now, and I hesitated. The footsteps stopped a few
feet away. I grabbed a book and closed the door. I saw
that it was the wrong book, and I had to fumble through
my combination and open the door again. Whoever it
was, was still there. I shifted the rearview mirror and

looked right into the green-shadowed, black-rimmed, blue mascaraed brown eyes of Miss Epler, the new English teacher with the crooked nose and the perfect, freshly bleached Sassoon haircut.

"Are you okay, Debbie?" she asked.

I nodded. Miss Epler clip-clopped over and stood next to me. Even in platform shoes, she was shorter than I was.

"Are you sick?" she asked.

I shook my head, still looking straight ahead at the neat stack of books.

"Do you want to talk about it?" she asked.

The muscles in my face were trying to seize up, a bucketful of tears was pressing against the backs of my eyes, and working their way up through my windpipe were some heaving sobs, which I knew would be loud and embarrassing. I gave a tiny shrug, and one of the sobs escaped, sounding like a heavy piece of furniture being dragged across the floor.

Miss Epler put her hands on my shoulders. "Come on," she said. "I have a free period."

She gently closed my locker door and led me down the hall. She left me outside the teachers' lounge and returned in a minute with a bag of corn chips and two bottles of Squirt. "This is probably not very nutritious," she said, "but there's not much choice in there."

We sat on the front steps of the school. Miss Epler ripped open the bag of chips and started crunching, but when she noticed I wasn't eating any, she tried to muffle her crunching. Then she stopped, licked the salt from her fingers, and took a sip of her Squirt.

"So, what's up?" she said. "Let me guess. Boys. You had a fight with your boyfriend."

"No," I said. "I don't have one."

"Good for you, you're better off," she said. "I don't have one either, but that's another story. Let's see . . . not a boyfriend. Hmm . . . Animal, vegetable, or mineral?"

I thought for a moment. "Is slime mold an animal or a vegetable?" I asked.

"Slime mold?" she repeated. "Your locker didn't look that bad to me. I've seen a lot worse."

"Not my locker," I said. "A person."

"Aaahhh," she said. "A person. Then animal, of course. But I'm pretty sure that mold is vegetable, so you need to pick a different analogy."

"Snake," I said. "No—worm."

"Wow," said Miss Epler. "Does this person have any good qualities?"

"No," I said. It felt very good to say it, but I knew it might not be completely fair. I didn't want to be fair, but in case God or anyone was listening, I added, "Some people think she does."

"Some people think she does," said Miss Epler. "That's good. Some objectivity." She took another chip and went on. "Now we can come back in a minute to how crappy this person is, but just for the sake of objectivity: What are the good qualities that some people think she has?"

This was one of those questions that English teachers like to ask, like: What three things would you take with you into the nuclear holocaust? Or, who should get off the lifeboat, you or Mahatma Gandhi? I wasn't in the mood for it right now, but with the promise of trashing Glenna just ahead, I scraped together the few nonnegative qualities of hers that I could think of.

"She's punctual," I said. "And clean. And neat."

"Hmm," said Miss Epler. "Punctual, clean, and neat. What else?"

I didn't feel like playing this game anymore. I said, "She took my friend away from me. I don't like her."

"Okay," said Miss Epler. "I see."

The air was humid and heavy and crammed with the grating sounds of jackhammers, bulldozers, and cement mixers from Birdvale. They were building a 650-foot-high smokestack at the power plant, so that the fly ash would float farther away before settling to the earth and landing on someone else's town.

"You know," said Miss Epler, "maybe this person didn't take your friend away from you."

"Yes, she did," I shot back.

"Maybe partly," she said carefully. "But at least partly it was your friend who left. All by herself. I just think that if you're going to be angry, you should be angry at the right person."

It was my friend who left.

All by herself.

A black pit opened inside me, and I fell in. I fell and I fell.

When I stopped falling, my face and my hands and my knees were warm and wet with tears, and the cold stone step I was sitting on was making me numb. I felt Miss Epler's hands squeezing my shoulders, and I heard her murmuring, "It's okay, it's okay, you're going to be all right, it's okay, I mean, I know it certainly doesn't *feel* okay right now, but you *will* be okay."

My breath was coming in jerky sobs, evening out only to collapse again. Finally, I got my breathing to calm down. In, out, in, out. No loud noises. I lifted my head, and my glasses slid down to the tip of my tear-slicked nose. I dried them with my skirt, then used my sleeve to wipe my face, but I needed something else to blow my nose.

"Here," said Miss Epler. She handed me some Kleenex. She was watching me with a concerned expression.

"It's a good thing I'm not the guidance counselor," she said. "The whole school would be bawling. Everyone would have to wear life jackets.

"Listen," she said. "It's almost time for the bell. Let's go in and wash your face." She took me into the teachers' washroom and put wet paper towels on my face and drops of Visine in my eyes.

"This is how all the stars do it," she said. And then: "Maybe just a little blusher," brushing some pink onto my cheeks. "You want eye shadow? You would look stunning in lavender, but you have too much on your mind today to be fighting off advances. Let's just use a little concealer to deblotchify you." I let her pat something around my eyes, her bracelets bangling and clacking together on her arm. She was trying to jolly me up, and her voice was calming, but when she led me to the mirror, I looked like death with rosy cheeks.

"Now, take a deep breath," she said, "and if anyone asks, you have hay fever. I think there's still some ragweed out there. And if there isn't, who cares, right?"

I wondered how long this hay fever season would be lasting.

We stepped out of the washroom, and the bell rang.

"Hang in there, kiddo," said Miss Epler. She gave my arm another squeeze. "Are you going to be okay?" I tried to smile but didn't even come close. I felt tears welling up again.

"You are," she said. "You are absolutely going to be okay. Okay? I'll see you sixth period."

The wave of voices and footsteps swelled and burst through the classroom doors into the hallway. I let myself be carried back to my locker, where I messed up the combination three times before getting it right. I slipped back into the current that was pulsing up the stairs and ejected myself into life science class. For once I was grateful that alphabetical order kept me on the far side of the room from where Maureen and Glenna would sit.

I opened my notebook and didn't look up when I heard their voices entering the room. I wasn't ready to look at anyone. My eyes and my heart felt thick and swollen. Paul Nepovicz was sitting in front of me, and I stared at the back of his shirt. It was paisley, in psychedelic rainbow colors. It must have put me into some sort of a hypnotic state because suddenly Linda Sabotnik was passing a note to my desk that said, "Do you like Paul N.?" I considered this for a second, then looked at her as if to say, Are you nuts? She pointed to my notebook. I saw that I had copied his whole paisley shirt. I wrote, "No,

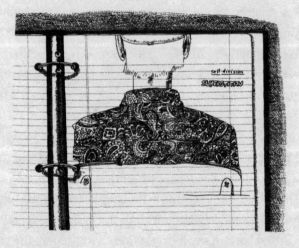

just his shirt," on the note and passed it back. Linda passed another note that said, "Where were you last period?" I wrote back, "Nurse's office. Bad hay fever." I looked back at my notebook page. Besides Paul Nepovicz's shirt, neck, and ears, there were the words *cell division* and *superstition,* but I had no idea what Mr. Zianetti had talked about. I wrote, "Can I copy your notes?" and passed it to Linda.

I didn't have a plan. I was just putting one foot in front of the other. I moved like the wrong end of a magnet through the iron filings of the day, repelling contact. I could feel Maureen's questioning glances. I could sense Glenna's satisfaction. She was so sure I was out of the picture that she came over and, in a voice that almost sounded friendly, asked me if I was going to lunch. As if you cared, I thought.

"I can't," I lied. "I have a doctor's appointment."

"Are you sick?" she asked with fake sympathy.

Only of you, popped spitefully into my mind. But aloud I said, "Just hay fever. Allergies."

"I didn't know you had allergies," she said.

"Neither did I," I said. "But I'm starting to think I might."

I wanted Maureen to come to her senses and say, "You, Debbie, are my best and truest friend. I'm so sorry, Glenna, but you will have to go back to the pond scum where you belong."

She didn't. She didn't say anything like that.

I started to understand that she wasn't going to. Ever. I was adrift. I wondered what I had done wrong. What was wrong with me. Why my friend had left. All by herself. I wanted to ask her why. I wanted to ask, How? But something I had thought was solid was just gone. It had dissolved, and I couldn't bring myself to ask anymore.

I walked to school by myself. I was starting to get used to it when one day a voice called out to me from behind, "Hey. Debbie. Wait up." I turned around. It was Marie Prbyczka. I waited for her to catch up.

"Don't you hang out with Maureen no more?" she asked. "Did you'ns have a fight or something?"

"No, we're still friends," I said. This wasn't exactly true, but I still didn't feel like saying so.

"I thought you guys were like this." She crossed her fingers, like for good luck or telling a fib. "Me and Don used to say to each other, 'Oh, look, here comes the Bobbsey Twins.'"

Part of me was proud, but another part was embarrassed and sent blood rushing to my face and ears. This must be some evolutionary survival mechanism, but I can't imagine how it worked. I also can't imagine Marie reading *The Bobbsey Twins*. Probably she just knew the title. I was surprised they had even paid any attention to us.

"Where's Don?" I asked her. "Doesn't he usually give you a ride?"

"That jagoff," she said. "He has some new girlfriend. Some chick from Hesmont. I told him, 'If you're calling her up, don't bother calling me up no more.'" She didn't seem to be heartbroken. She didn't even seem to be concerned.

"Do you miss him?" I asked.

Marie laughed. "I miss getting a ride to school," she said.

Marie was all right to walk with. She talked a lot, so I didn't have to. She told me about Jerome and Anthony, the oldest of her little brothers, who were always stealing her cigarettes and then almost setting the house on fire. She told me stories about the weekend dances at the Hesarena. The stories always had cigarettes, beer, cars with a lot of people packed in, and fights. Sometimes the police. I wondered what it would be like to go there. Marie talked as if I would be doing that, any day now. I sort of hoped that I wouldn't be. I sort of hoped some other option might come along.

One day Marie told me that her dad had girlfriends besides her mother, that they both drank too much sometimes and then they had arguments where they threw things. The gold grapes flying though the air, the lamp with the figurines.

"At each other?" I asked her.

"No," Marie said. "Just across the room or at the wall or something. Just to make some noise."

I looked over at her. She was staring straight ahead, out from under her long bangs, out from behind her beige makeup that ended like a mask at her chin and the sides of her face. Her eyes were watery. Then she turned to me. She peered out through the mascara and said, "I bet that don't happen at your house."

"No," I said. I couldn't even imagine it.

Marie sighed. "My dad is such a jagoff," she said. "I can't wait till I'm eighteen."

It turned out that Bobby Prbyczka was in Mom's class at school in September. And in October and November, of course, until the Prbyczkas drove off into nowhere in their big, shiny car. A few weeks into school Bobby started showing up in clothes that didn't seem to have been washed lately. Then they were the same clothes day after day.

"I feel sorry for him," Mom said. "He actually smells, and the other kids don't want to be around him."

She gave Bobby a bag, and she told him to put his dirty clothes into it and bring it over to our house. She washed them, folded them, and ironed the shirts and pants. Some things she even mended. At school one day she had Bobby stay inside for recess, and she helped him to wash himself. In minutes the water in the sink was a dark gray.

"Good Lord, Bobby," she said, "when was the last time you took a bath?"

"I think we're out of soap," he said. "And anyways, my dad don't make us take baths."

"Oh, he doesn't, does he? Well, what about your mother? What does she say about that?"

"She don't say nothing. She ain't there."

This stopped my mom in her tracks. But not for long. "Where is she?" she asked Bobby.

It turned out that the Prbyczkas were separated. Mr. P. said it was his damn house and he wasn't going to move out, so Mrs. P. was staying with her sister for now, until she could find a place where there was room for the kids.

Mom started packing Bobby a lunch, and she made him eat half of it before school started. She made him brush his teeth. "I can't feed the whole family," she said, "but it's hard to teach when you can hear someone's stomach growling."

One day Mom opened Bobby's laundry bag and pulled out four or five shirts. Men's shirts. "Well, if he thinks I'm going to do *his* laundry," she said, and she stuffed them back in the bag.

When I asked Marie if it was true, she rolled her eyes casually and said, "Yeah, her and my dad had a fight. So what else is new? They think they're Liz and Richard. She'll stay at my aunt Renée's for a couple weeks. Then my dad will show up there with flowers or something, and she'll come back."

She stopped walking, put a finger to her lips, and narrowed her eyes. Then she brightened a little and said, "Huh. It's lasting longer than usual this time. Maybe they really will split up."

CHAPTER EIGHT

I WROTE a story for English class in which all the main characters died horrible deaths. At the same time I was writing an extremely optimistic story for science class that was a lot of work because it had to use three scientific facts as plot elements, and it had to be sort of technically accurate.

By the time I got to the English one, which was supposed to have a tragic hero with a "fatal flaw," I had to hurry. I went for broken hearts, fatal diseases, car accidents, and poisonings. And a drowning. The fatal flaw of my heroine was forgetfulness. She kept forgetting to return phone calls, look both ways, label containers correctly, etc. She forgot to bring the life jackets. Finally, she forgot to bring food on a camping trip, and she starved, alone and forgotten (Irony. Also poetic justice) in the wilderness. I knew it wasn't a great story, I was just trying to show that I got the point: Fatal flaw → Tragedy.

It took me by surprise when Miss Epler leaned over my desk a few days later and asked me to come back to the classroom after school. "Just for a few minutes," she said. "I want to talk to you about your paper."

"Oh. Sure," I said. But before I could read her expression or ask any questions, she was off on the other side of the room. The bell rang, the class swarmed up in a mob between us, and I decided I could wait to find out what she wanted. Probably I had been just too quick and sloppy. Then I had another idea: Maybe my story was good, really good. Maybe she wanted to send it off somewhere.

When I got there, Miss Epler was at her desk, reading. I chose a nearby desk and waited. Miss Epler looked up and smiled her V-shaped, peach-colored smile. "Hey, Debbie," she said.

This seemed like a good start.

I smiled, too, and said, "Hi."

"So, how are things going for you?" she asked casually.

I shrugged. "All right," I said.

"Yeah?" she asked.

"Yeah," I said.

"*Really* all right?" she asked. She leaned back in her chair and looked thoughtfully into my eyes, toward my soul. I looked back. I tried to be thoughtful, too, but my mind wandered to how lavender eye shadow, or any color really, doesn't look as good at the end of the day when a person's eyes start to get red and watery. Probably this is even caused by bits of powder flaking off and falling in.

I snapped back into focus and said, "I'm okay. I'm fine."

"Your story," said Miss Epler, "seemed a little angry. A little morbid."

"It did?" I said.

She nodded. "Perhaps because every single character dies," she said. "In awful ways."

"Wasn't that the idea, though?" I asked. "Tragedy?"

"Tragedy, yes. Apocalypse, no. You might want to leave one teeny-tiny shred of hope and redemption, just for contrast."

"Oh," I said. "Okay."

Miss Epler seemed to be waiting for more. I thought I knew what, so I said, "Do you want me to write it over?"

But she shook her head. "No. I know you could. I'm not worried about that. What worries me is that someone who writes such a story might actually be feeling, well . . . somewhat unhappy."

That was one I hadn't thought of. I leaned forward on

my elbows. There was an
owl's face in the fake wood
grain on the desktop. Almost
all fake wood grain has an
owl's face in it somewhere.
I traced it with a finger.

"It's just a story," I said.
"It doesn't mean anything."

"Stories don't mean anything?" asked Miss Epler after
a pause.

More carefully then, I said, "Not all of them."

She clasped her hands to her chest, raised her eyes,
and said, "I think I can feel my heart breaking!"

She was joking, and I relaxed a little and smiled. I
thought we were moving out of the serious part. But Miss
Epler turned thoughtful again and asked, "By the way,
how did that friend thing work out? The one with the—
what was she? A centipede or a slug or something?
Something horrible. How is that going?"

I looked down at the plastic wood grain again. I reached
for my pencil to draw in the rest of the owl, then decided
I'd better not. I wasn't thinking about the friend thing. I
was keeping it in a separate compartment, with the door
shut. There was a lot a person could do by herself. Like
read. At least in books there were people who were faithful even unto death, people who didn't just forget about
each other for no reason that you could think of.

"It's okay," I said.

There was a hesitant knock on the door frame. Alice Dahlpke was standing there.

"Oh, hi, Alice!" said Miss Epler. "Come on in and join us."

Alice tippy-tapped over and lowered herself into a desk. She twirled some strands of hair around a finger and raised the corners of her mouth in an uncertain smile.

"Well, here we all are," said Miss Epler brightly. Then, as if she had just remembered something, she checked her watch and said, "Oh, my. Listen, I have to go make a very quick phone call. Do you mind? Can you hang on for a few minutes? I'll be right back. You girls chat."

She whirled out of the room and clip-clopped down the hall. There was the thud of a heavy door falling shut, then quiet.

The room was still. Afternoon sunlight poured in silently under the yellowed shades. It gave an intricate golden edge to the hunched-over shape of Alice examining her split ends.

"So," I said, "what was your story about?"

"A nuclear war," she said.

"Does everyt...y die?" I asked her.

"All except the mutants," she said.

"We were supposed to leave a shred of hope," I said. "For contrast."

Alice seemed surprised. "Mutants can be hopeful," she said. "Mutation is a way of surviving."

"That might be true for viruses, but I'm not sure it's exactly true for people," I said. "Although maybe if you explain the scientific part . . ." Suddenly I had a realization. "Did you use this same story for science?"

Alice nodded.

"You creep! Why didn't I think of that?"

Alice smiled one of her huge smiles. (Here is how Alice's outside appearance is like her insides: untidy and murky, with bright and dazzling flashes, which are her smiles on the outside—almost embarrassing in their wideness and joyfulness—and her understanding of subjects like math and science on the inside. Under her mousy brown strings of hair lives a great intelligence. Geometry is candy for Alice, but everyday life is a foreign country to her. Sometimes even walking looks like something she is trying out for the first time.)

We sat there for a few minutes, waiting. I hummed and looked around the room. Alice held herself tensely, as if she would love to drum her fingers or jiggle her foot if only she could remember to do that.

"So," I said.

I didn't know what I was going to say next, but it seemed we might as well talk. I tried to think of something Alice and I had in common. I had to go pretty far back. "Do you remember that time in Girl Scouts when we went horseback riding?" I asked.

"Yes," said Alice.

"That was fun, wasn't it?" I said.

Alice smiled, but she didn't say anything. I had expected to get at least two or three minutes out of this topic. Where was Miss Epler anyway? I tried again. "I wish there were horses around here," I said. "I love horses."

"There's a horse farm in West Bird Township," said Alice.

"You're kidding," I said. "Where?"

Alice furrowed her dusky brow in thought and pulled

the tips of hair she was sucking on from the corner of her mouth. "Somewhere out by that greenhouse on Walters Road. We've driven by it in the car."

This piece of information pierced me like an arrow. I had spent whole years of my life, in grade school, reading over and over again about the Godolphin Arabian, Black Beauty, National Velvet, and all those ponies out on Chincoteague. I had dreamed of riding bareback over the dark moors or through the pounding surf at sunrise, but except for that one long-ago Girl Scout field trip, which was pretty short and pretty tame, I had hardly even been near a horse. How could I not have known that there were horses right in West Bird Township? Why hadn't anyone ever told me?

At first I felt cheated. But then a different feeling, like putting on old clothes and finding money in the pockets, took over, and I was filled with a desire to see those horses.

"Do you think you could find it?" I asked Alice. "Do you want to go there, on a hike?"

And that is how I found myself, one Saturday in October, hiking to West Bird Township with Alice Dahlpke.

I should mention that Miss Epler was thrilled when she returned to find us making plans. She seemed to forget why we had come; you would have thought the whole reason was to set up this hike. I didn't remind her of our crappy disaster stories, and fortunately Alice didn't either. Probably she had forgotten, too.

It dawned on me later that maybe that *was* why we were there: Miss Epler hoped that a friendship would spring up between Alice and me and rescue both of us from friendless despair. I didn't know why she thought we would be a good match. Maybe all alone people seem alike to a not-alone person. It was nice of her to try.

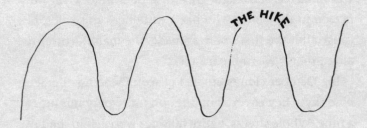

CHAPTER NINE

THE HIKE

W<small>E HAD</small> apples, so the horses would come close to us, and cookies. I wore my CPO jacket, which of course is not an actual CPO jacket like everyone else gets to wear ("They look sloppy," says my mother), but more like a heavy wool pullover shirt with a loop and button at the neck.

regular
C. P. O.   mine

It used to belong to my cousin Mike, and when I wear it, I feel not only warm but also athletic and adventurous. I don't know what Alice was wearing, probably something shapeless and colorless. Actually, if I think about it, she was probably wearing green pants that were too short, thin socks sliding down into beat-up blue Keds, a striped windbreaker, and a light gray turtleneck. Alice is the only person in the world who has a turtleneck this color, because after the first one was made, the manufacturer realized that it was a big mistake.

Big October clouds ambled peacefully across the deep blue sky. They covered up the sun for twenty minutes at a time. Whole streets, entire hillsides were left in shadow. Then the sun would pop out, and the shadow would be peeled back down the street, across the hillside. We decided it would be quicker to cut through the woods, so down we skidded, hopping and tripping over roots and fallen branches all the way to the bottom, where the creek trickled along next to the railroad tracks. Partway up the next hill we sat on a rock in a passing patch of sunlight and looked back at our town. Because now we were in Birdvale. The trees and rooftops of Seldem looked so tranquil, so orderly. The cookies were store-bought oatmeal with the marshmallow cream in between and tasted exquisite.

"Do you like that new song in chorus?" I asked Alice.

She thought for a moment, then started to sing. I sang, too. I love singing in harmony, even with a wobbly soprano like Alice. She is wobbly but fearless. My own voice is unexceptional but reliable, which is all anyone expects from an alto. The song we were singing there on the rock was a semidopey one called "The Stars That

Guide the Voyager," but it had some good parts, like the long, tricky run on the word *be*.

can   be-e-e-e-e-e-e-e-e-e-e-e-e-e-e-e-e-e-e-e-e-e-e-e-e-e-e-e-e-e-e-e-e-e-e-e-e-e-e-e-e-e-e-e-e-e-e-e-e,

Lots of different notes, no place to take a breath, hard to do. After that we did "Adoramus Te," which makes everyone feel like a vocal champion because it's simple, and not too high, but sounds mysterious and holy and is in Latin. Then it was time to stand up and move again.

As we crested the hill, we were startled to see more hills rising in front of us. For some reason we both thought Bird Township would be right there. We kept going, though, down and up, down and up, down and up until finally we came to an open field. On the far side were a few houses. We had been walking for a couple of hours now, and I wondered if Alice knew where we were.

"How much farther do you think it is?" I asked her, to find out.

"It's taking longer than I thought," she said, "but we should be getting close."

She stopped. She looked carefully in every direction. I looked, too, and then I watched Alice looking. I think that Alice will someday solve problems that have baffled humankind for centuries. But they are not going to be problems like: Where are we, where is the horse farm, and how do we get home without climbing any more hills?

"Let's head for those telephone poles," I said. "There's probably a road there."

We crossed the muddy field and caught a tiny glimpse of Birdvale High School. The telephone poles were planted alongside an unfamiliar country road. We walked in the direction of the school.

"Do you think the horses are between here and the school?" I asked Alice.

"No," said Alice thoughtfully.

"Let's eat the apples then," I said.

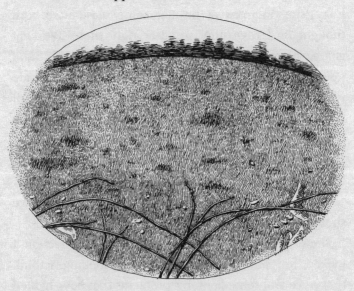

A little while later we walked past the empty parking lot of the empty high school into the streets of Birdvale.

It felt exotic to be there on foot, with nothing but feet to get us home again. We had been to most of the stores, and some of the houses, in cars, and they were a lot like the stores and houses in Seldem. At the moment, though, they seemed somehow more interesting. We reached the block of stores where the bakery was, between the hardware store and the doll hospital.

"Do you have any money?" I asked Alice. We fished in our pockets for change. I had some; Alice didn't.

"I'll treat," I said, and we went inside the bakery. Fans hanging from the high old ceiling turned slowly, wafting heavenly smells all around. Paper cutouts of jack-o'-lanterns and autumn leaves were Scotch-taped to the walls. We looked at every tray before deciding. I chose a cream puff, and Alice selected a flaky apple turnover. It was turning into a day of great eating, and we walked along Pittsfield Street, silently savoring our personal pastry paradises while trucks and cars whizzed by. Alice had little flecks of apple turnover on her lips and chin.

"Do I have any crumbs on my face?" I asked her.

"No," she said. "Do I?"

"Just a couple," I said, and brushed them off.

Pittsfield Street was long, dirty, and noisy, but eventually it led us under the railroad trestle and into Seldem. We were running out of steam. The late-afternoon shadows were horizontal and blue. Alice told me about a book she was reading about snails. I could read a magazine article about snails, but not a whole book. Alice was telling me only the most interesting parts, though, like how some people eat them. I guess the pastry made her think of it. We got to my house and said good-bye.

I walked around to the back door since my shoes were covered with dried mud. I breathed in the chilly autumn air and felt the achiness of my muscles as they prepared to collapse. I felt something else, too. I felt happy. I felt good. Without Maureen.

"Hmm," I said aloud. The thought of Maureen threw a shadow over my heart. But I slipped out from under it. Not today, I thought. Not right now.

The sun was about to set, bathing the world in a golden light. Including my mother's face, looking through the window of the back door, golden and rosy. Golden and rosy and furious.

"Where on earth have you been," she said, opening the door.

It wasn't exactly a question, and I knew there wasn't exactly an answer, not one that would be good enough. "We got lost," I said. "We were lucky to find our way home."

THEN SOMETHING else happened.

It was a Tuesday evening. Mom and Dad had gone out somewhere, and Chrisanne and I were home by ourselves, watching TV. We had made ourselves big sundaes with chocolate and caramel syrup, walnuts and chocolate chips, and Cupcake was sitting up between us, waiting for his turn. Chrisanne finished first.

She put her bowl down for Cupcake and went upstairs to take a bath. I was already in my PJs, with my hair rolled around orange juice cans on top of my head.

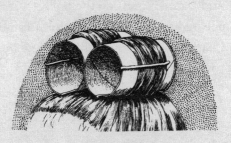

to make it straighter

A minute later Chrisanne came hurrying back down the stairs. I looked up from my ice cream as she tripped on the bottom step and knocked over the pole lamp. Nothing broke, but Cupcake jumped up and ran barking out of the room.

"Are you okay?" I asked.

As she picked herself (and the lamp) up, she answered in an urgent whisper, "There's a man in our bathroom! We have to get out of the house!"

"Oh. Sure," I said. I sat back and took another bite of ice cream. Practically every time our parents go out, Chrisanne hears some noise and makes me check all the closets while she stands at the front door, ready to escape at my first scream.

"No!" she insisted. "There really is!" She glanced nervously up the stairs and squatted next to my chair with her face about ten inches from mine. She was making just enough sounds like *t*'s and *s*'s to make it a little easier than pure lipreading.

"I saw his coat and his shoes. He's standing behind the bathroom door. I turned on the light and tried to push the door all the way open, and it wouldn't go. Then I looked in the crack, and I could see the chest of his coat and his shoes. We have to get out of here. We have to go to Fran and Danny's and call the police!"

She disappeared into the kitchen, the storm door fell shut with a bang, and her blurred form flew by outside the dining room window.

The chest of someone's coat and shoes—this was more convincing. I quickly assessed the situation: I had to get Cupcake and myself out of the house, but I didn't know where he had gone. I wasn't about to walk past the bathroom door to look for him. I wanted to let the man in the bathroom know that everyone was leaving the house, but I also wanted him to think we didn't know he was there. So that if he had any sense at all, he would just wait a few minutes till we were gone. Then he could burgle our house in peace without kidnapping or shooting anyone.

"Cupcake!" I called out, loudly but calmly. "It's nine o'clock. Time for us to go over to Fran's house. We're all supposed to go over to Fran's house now. Chrisanne's already over there. Come on, Cupcake!"

Cupcake jingled back into the room. I picked him up and carried him, squirming and struggling, as I announced, "Here we go, Cupcake. Over to Fran and Danny's house. *No one here now. Here we all go!*"

My footsteps were slow and even across the back porch, but when I hit the grass, I bolted. I was pretty sure the intruder couldn't see me from the bathroom window, especially in the dark.

Tesey and Chrisanne were waiting, and they pulled me, with Cupcake, into the kitchen and locked the door behind me. Fran was already on the phone, talking to the police. "Yes," she said. "In the bathroom, up on the second floor. One of the girls saw him. . . . Yes, both of them are here with me now. Next door." She paused, listening. "That's right. Thank you."

She hung up the phone, and then, suddenly, someone was jiggling the knob of the kitchen door, trying to get it open. We all shrieked and flew together in a huddle. Fran positioned herself defiantly between us and the door, which was now being banged upon. Cupcake hid bravely behind her, barking and wagging his tail.

"Get down on the floor!" she bellowed. Then, more reassuringly: "The police will be here in no time. And we have a very good lock on that door."

"Open the door, Frances!" It was the voice of Danny, Fran's husband.

"Oh, cripes," said Fran. "It's Danny. He went down to the store for milk." She slid the chain off to let him in, then locked it again.

"What's going on?" said Danny.

Before Fran could explain, the front doorbell rang, and a deep voice announced, "Police!"

Tesey and Chrisanne and I were still crouching on the kitchen floor to avoid any bullets that might come flying through the windows. We stayed there while Fran spoke briefly to the policemen, who seemed to fill up the living room, though they were trying hard to fit on the foot-wiping rug by the door. After she sent them next door, we crawled up onto chairs and waited nervously. Fran filled a plate with cookies and slices of nut bread.

"Should I make more coffee?" she said to Danny. Then

she said, "Our policemen are so excellent. Did you see how fast they got here? It didn't take them five minutes."

Cupcake's toenails clicked back and forth across the linoleum. He was keeping an eye on both doors. Danny sat down at the table with us and picked up a biscotti.

"I'd have a cup of coffee," he said to Fran. Then to Chrisanne he said, "So, tell me what happened now, sweetie."

Chrisanne told the story again, and by this time the intruder was wearing a tweed coat (probably stolen), and she thought he had looked at her through the crack in the door, but she had pretended not to see him before walking calmly down the stairs and leading Cupcake and me out of the house. I was getting ready to comment on the "calmly" part when the policemen returned to the front door.

Fran spoke to them for a few minutes, then came back into the kitchen for Chrisanne. "You're going to come back and stay with us until your mom and dad get home," she said gently. "But the policemen want to show you what it was that you saw."

Tesey and I looked at each other in suspense as the policemen led Chrisanne out of the house. . . .

My mother had been in a hurry that evening. She had taken a quick bath to freshen up, dried off, and sprinted to her bedroom to dress herself. It was unusual, a once-in-a-lifetime event, for my mom to leave her clothes in the bathroom, but that's what she'd done. She left her

Hush Puppy shoes on the floor, neatly placed side by side, perpendicular to the wall. Her gray wool slacks hung from the hook on the back of the door, bulged out a little by the blouse underneath them.

Look, you'll see what I mean: Chrisanne and Cupcake and I had made a dramatic escape from the threat of wool slacks and Hush Puppies.

The policemen were nice. They told Chrisanne that she had done exactly the right thing. One of them said he had teenage daughters of his own, and he would want them to get out of the house, too, if they ever even *suspected* that someone might be in there. Then I guess he went home and told the teenage daughters, when he could stop laughing for long enough to speak, all about us and how he had rescued us from our mom's pants and shoes.

The news spread like wildfire. You would think there would be some kind of law about confidentiality, but overnight Chrisanne and I became semifamous persons. This is not hard to do in Seldem, where you can become famous for having a hangnail. I was glad I could blame the whole thing on Chrisanne, but even so, by lunchtime

I was looking forward to college, where I hoped no one would know about it. I wondered if I would have to go out of state. I carried my tray into the cafeteria and looked around for a hiding place.

"Hey, Debbie, look out!" someone yelled. "There's a pair of pants behind you!" It was Steven Heber and some of his dopey companions, sitting at the table in front of me. Well, when someone shouts, "Look out!" it's only natural for a person to jump a little bit. So I jumped. This was good for a few more peals of merry laughter. I bristled and walked past as if I had places to go and people to meet. Through the noise and the lukewarm brown fog of Meat Cup, I moved toward the table where Alice Dahlpke was sitting with Connie Klemenko and Jane Haslett.

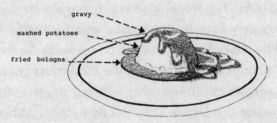

I was just cutting into my Meat Cup when a voice nearby said, "Debbie!"

I turned to see Patty Tsimmicz, who was sitting with the next clump of people at the table. "Hi," I said.

"Hi," Patty said back. Then she said, "Listen, I just wanted to tell you that it wasn't me who told about what happened at your house. It was my sister, Diane."

"What?" I said.

"My dad was one of the policemen," she said. "I wouldn't have told anyone, but Diane is kind of a blabbermouth."

"Oh," I said. "That's all right." What else could I say?

"You have to admit, though," said Patty, a smile coming to her lips. "It's a good story."

I braced myself to bristle, but then something happened. A lot of times when people say, "We're not laughing at you, we're laughing with you," it just isn't all that convincing. But Patty's smile seemed to say, "Hey, crazy things happen all the time, to everyone. Isn't it funny?"

I had to smile, too. "You should have seen it," I said. And as I told her the whole story, her laughter and then mine made it funnier than it probably even was. Suddenly I didn't feel stupid anymore. It was like the flying-up ceremony back in Girl Scouts, where all of us little Brownies walked over a wooden bridge set in the middle of the floor in the basement of the Presbyterian church, and when we got to the other side and stepped off, we were Junior Girl Scouts. Only this time Patty had helped me over an imaginary bridge from Stupidland to the Land of Knowing a Good Joke.

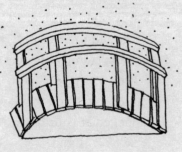

A couple of days later the phone rang at our house, but I didn't hear it. Or I didn't notice it, because I had forgotten that a ringing phone might ever have anything to do with me; it was just another sound, like a car going by on the street or the heater coming on in the basement.

I didn't even notice the first few times Chrisanne called my name. I was sitting on the bedroom floor, listening to Chrisanne's records and knitting an eight-foot-long scarf, in burgundy and cream stripes.

I did hear a pounding on the stairs just before Chrisanne burst through the door, said, "Debbietelephone," and bounded back down to sit on the couch next to her new boyfriend, Dale. I figured somebody needed a babysitter and followed her down, wondering whose kids I would be giving baths to that evening.

But it was Patty, Patty Tsimmicz. She was inviting me to go to a movie. Maybe get pizza after.

I said, "Sure."

I hung up the phone. I looked at it for a minute. I rose onto my tiptoes. I bent my knees and did some dance-type leaps and spins around the dining room table and into the living room. I sang some opera notes for Chrisanne and Dale as I walked past them and out onto the porch. It was an exceptional day out there. Huge, wild gusts of wind were hurling the rain sideways, in buckets. Yellow leaves were being slapped onto the wet sidewalk and the street in tangled, cheery patterns. I worked my hands Chinese style into the opposite sleeves of my sweatshirt and watched some cars go by with their lights beaming out bright tunnels of raindrops, their wheels spinning silvery plumes of spray into the air. I was getting wet, not from the cars but from the rain blowing in under the porch roof. I inhaled one more gulp of the beautiful, cold, damp air and went back inside to the also beautiful dryness and warmth.

Something good was happening.

CHAPTER ELEVEN

SOMETIME IN October Marie had found another boyfriend with a car to drive her to school. Larry Hlotva was
the only ninth grader who already had a driver's license.
He was sixteen. He was big and bulky. He and Marie
lurched around school with Marie tucked under Larry's
armpit. This can't have been all that pleasant for Marie,
but she didn't seem to mind. She was wearing his chain
and a fake class ring wrapped in angora yarn. They were
"going together."

PROOFS
OF A
BOYFRIEND

— fresh angora every
day to match outfit

Shown at
½ actual size

Larry's hair was the color of cornsilk, with sulfury highlights. It hung down over his ears in a limp, wavy helmet, and his bangs flipped up like a visor, just at eye level. Downy blond hairs sprouted over his lip and here and there across the pale, pocky skin of his puffy face. A group of them had burst through at his chin. Looks-wise, he was a few steps down the ladder from Don, but maybe he was nicer, who knows?

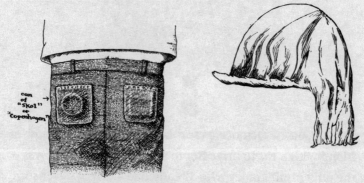

Larry's back and hair-do

Marie and I still said hi, but I didn't see her much outside Larry's armpit. When I did see her, I didn't think that she might be unhappy. I mean, I knew that her mother was living somewhere else and that she had big problems with her dad and some junior juvenile delinquent brothers. Maybe Larry Hlotva was "any port in a storm." But I thought Marie could handle whatever came along. I thought of her as someone who did whatever she wanted to. That's what she would have said. She skipped school a lot, and when she did come, no one seemed to care what she did. The principals and teachers at school had already given up on Marie. They hardly even saw her, except as some kind of blemish. She could have stood on her head wearing a burlap bag, and nobody would have noticed it all that much. They thought she was stupid. She wasn't stupid.

One Saturday in November, I saw the FOR SALE sign in the Prbyczkas' front yard. Someone had mowed the grass, but everything else looked as ratty as ever. The car was not in the driveway, but I thought I saw someone moving past the window, and I thought it was Marie. All of a sudden I felt like talking to her. So I walked up the sidewalk and knocked. I stood there for a minute waiting. Then I heard footsteps, and Marie opened the door. No one else seemed to be at home. Marie wasn't wearing makeup, and I was surprised to see that she had freckles and fresh, clear skin. Her eyes looked naked and shy. She invited me in and offered me a pop.

I followed her from room to room with my glass of pop. She was packing the clothes of all the Prbyczka kids in boxes. There wasn't much to pack, and most of what there was, was scattered on the floor or hanging from doorknobs.

"But you just moved here," I said. "Where are you going?"

"Pine Township," she said. It wasn't that far away, but it was a different school. Probably I would not see her much. Maybe not at all. Maybe never.

There was a crescent-shaped redness just below Marie's lower lip. It looked raw or sore, like an injury. I was about to ask her what it was, or how it happened, when she bit down onto it, in a quick, nervous movement, like biting your fingernails. I looked away, down to where her hands were putting a little pair of slippers into a box.

"At least you won't have to live with your dad anymore," I said.

"I wish," she said. "Him and my mom are back together. They're acting like lovebirds. That should last a couple weeks." She tossed a balled-up sock into the box.

"Oh," I said. "So why are you moving then?"

Marie shrugged. "We can't afford this place, I guess," she said. "I don't care, though. People here are boring. And stuck up. Not you. But most of them are." She sat down on one of the beds and tapped a cigarette out of a pack that was lying there. She lit it and took a puff.

"You should see the dump we're moving into," she said. "You have to go outside to turn around." She grinned and knocked some ash into an empty glass on the windowsill. "My mom is calling it a cottage," she said, "but if you ask me, that's just another word for rathole."

She squinted at the smoke from her cigarette gracefully unfurling in a shaft of sunlight and dust in the still air. Her face was the face of a little kid under the spell of soap bubbles. Bobby's face, only prettier. She drew her knees up inside her sweater. I leaned back on my hands.

We sat there watching the smoke make lazy, winding patterns.

The spell was broken by the sound of a car dragging its muffler down the street outside. Marie bit down on her lip again. I winced. She caught me looking at her, and something passed between us. Understanding or friendship or truth or something, I don't know quite what it was. Then, instantly, she was the usual Marie, breezy and tough. She crossed her legs and stubbed her cigarette out in the glass. "You don't have to feel sorry for me," she said. "I can take care of myself."

"I don't feel sorry for you," I lied, or half lied. And since one of the reasons that I felt sorry for her was Larry Hlotva, I asked, "Do you think you'll still go with Larry after you move?"

Marie nodded.

"Oh, yeah," she said. "He wants us to get married. We have to wait till I'm sixteen, but he can quit school next year and work at his cousin's garage."

This sounded like a really lousy idea, but then I wondered if my own probable future life as an old maid would be any better.

"Wow," I said. "I wonder if I'll even go out on a date by the time I'm sixteen."

Marie laughed. I liked making her laugh.

"Or ever," I said, and she laughed again.

"You will," she said. "It's too bad you have to wear glasses, though. Do you really need them?"

"Pretty much," I said. "But I'm hoping I can get contacts when I'm older."

"That will help," said Marie.

"I hope so," I said.

"It will," she insisted. "Take your glasses off for a minute."

I did.

"That's so much better. You should go without them."

"I kind of like being able to see, though," I said.

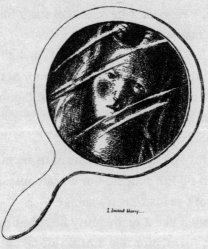

I looked blurry...

"What for?" said Marie.

A wave of voices floated into the house, then footsteps. Then the whole horde of Prbyczkas was inside. I helped carry boxes out to the car.

"Drop by and see us," said Mrs. P. "We love it when Marie's friends come to visit."

"Okay," I said, even though in the first place, I didn't

even know where it was, and in the second place, I had never even walked down the street to visit Marie, not before today. "Okay," I said. "Good luck."

"I'll miss you," I said to Marie. I meant it.

"Like fun you will," she said, but she was smiling.

Her dad smiled, too, through the windshield, a dazzling smile that I couldn't help smiling back at, even though I knew from Marie that he was kind of a jerk. Marie got in the front seat next to her mother and shut the door, muffling the noise from all the little Prbyczkas in the backseat to a dull roar, which faded to silence as the big car rolled down the street and disappeared around the corner.

At least until they reached Pine Township, the car would hold them all together. Who knew what would happen once they got out of it? The furniture was still there inside the house, but by the end of the day that was gone, too.

The street breathed a sigh of relief. The house waited like a scraped knee.

CHAPTER TWELVE

Thanksgiving Monday

"The thing is, I *liked* Marie," I said to Patty. We were walking down Pearl Avenue on Thanksgiving Monday, the first day of deer hunting. There was no school. We were going to Jim's Bargain Store for red thread, weather stripping, and green burlap. "So why did I, like, not be her friend? More than I did, I mean."

Patty thought it over. "Well, you're pretty different from each other," she said.

"Yeah, but can we be friends only with people who are just the same as us?" I asked. "Wouldn't that be sort of boring?"

"I don't think you have to be just the same," she said. "but there has to be something that's alike. Otherwise what do you do together? What do you talk about?"

We stopped to look at the revolving silver Christmas tree in the window of Tony Williams Shoes. Children's socks and slippers were hung on it like ornaments. The window on the other side had a New Year's Eve theme: a champagne bottle, confetti, and high-heeled patent leather shoes with buckles or ribbon roses or rhinestones that could be snapped on in front depending on the occasion or your mood.

Patty said, "I guess with anybody, there would be some things that are in common, just because you're both human beings. I mean, everyone has to eat and sleep. And breathe. Although breathing isn't something you usually talk about, unless for some reason somebody, like, *stops* breathing."

It was an interesting conversation, and it might have gone on for a lot longer, if I hadn't looked up just as we turned onto Pittsfield Street.

"That's George!" I said under my breath.

"What?" said Patty.

"That guy getting out of the car up there," I said, "I know him."

George circled to the passenger side and opened the door.

"And that's Mrs. Brown," I said as she stepped out onto the sidewalk, resplendent in sky blue ski pants and a white ski parka with a fur-lined hood. The ski parka had tags hanging from the zipper; leave it to people in

Deer Church to know where to find snow while the rest of us sputtered along in the drab gray nothing that hovers between autumn and real winter. George was wearing a car coat and a brown plaid scarf. He looked great, too, just because he was George.

"Who are they?" asked Patty.

"It's a long story," I said. "I'll tell you later."

Maybe later I could also explain why happiness was spurting up inside me at the sight of them.

"George!" I called out. "Mrs. Brown!"

They turned, and there was that moment that happens before someone recognizes you. It can happen with your own family, if you catch them off guard. I helped them out.

"I'm Debbie," I said. "I came to your garden last summer—"

"Of course!" said Mrs. Brown. "And we've been waiting for you to come back ever since."

"I knew I had connections in this town," said George.

"What are you doing in Seldem?" I asked.

"Pie," said Mrs. Brown. "Pie brings us here. George was kind enough to help me out with a big chore over in Plum Borough, and coming back, we decided the only way to keep up our strength and salvage the afternoon was to have some coffee and maybe a little dessert."

I noticed that we were all standing next to the Idle Hour Restaurant. "They do have really good pie here," I said.

George spoke to Patty. "I don't believe we've met," he said, "unless you have changed markedly."

She laughed. "I'm Patty," she said. "Patty Tsimmicz."

"Oops," I said. "I should have done that."

"Why don't you come in with us?" said Mrs. Brown. "Do you have the time? You can tell us which kind is the best."

So we did. Think about it, though. What are the chances that we would be walking by the Idle Hour at the exact moment George and Mrs. Brown stopped there? But there we were, ordering peach pie with ice cream in a booth with yellow vinyl seats. It felt like something that was supposed to happen. I felt that George and Mrs. Brown were people I was going to keep knowing somehow. It crossed my mind that if my mother had happened to see us sitting there, I would have had a hard time explaining how I knew them. What was I going to tell her when they showed up someday at my wedding? Well, that I could worry about later. But a reflex made me wipe the fog from the window and look out. That's when I saw what I almost didn't see that day, coming down the sidewalk. I saw Glenna and Maureen and a boy with his arm around Maureen's waist, and hers around his, girlfriend-boyfriend style.

Wow, I thought. Who's that?

Glenna's smile was pasted to her frozen face as she matched her pace to theirs. From behind her determined brightness peered the eyes of a frightened animal. They passed by our window, and, for an accidental instant Glenna's rattled eyes met mine. I wanted to feel satisfaction and revenge. But it was too much like looking into a mirror. I couldn't fit any spite into the small smile I tossed out like a tiny, halfhearted lifeline.

They walked by, and I scrambled back up onshore.

CHAPTER THIRTEEN

"We're all a little green around the gills," my mother said into the phone. She was still in her pink bathrobe and slippers. No makeup yet. She was telling Mrs. Schimpf we wouldn't be in church because of the flu. She winked at me as I took a package of English muffins out of the bread drawer. I was feeling better. And I was starved.

"Ed says he feels like he got hit with a Mack truck," Mom told Mrs. Schimpf.

My dad and Chrisanne were still upstairs in bed, limp washrags trying not to move. The house was dark and still, except for the light over the kitchen sink and the radio on low. The smell of my toasting English muffin filled the stale air with the promise of health and life, like the first crocus of spring. But it probably made Dad and

Chrisanne queasy. I needed to breathe some fresh air.

"I'm going for a walk, Mom," I said.

She tucked the phone under her chin and said quietly, "Okay, doll. Dress warm."

The whole world was gray and brown. Even if the brick chimneys had managed to reach a few inches higher and snag holes in the heavy clouds, there probably would have been more gray behind them. The trees in the front yards were bare. A few unraked brown leaves, curly and brittle, lay scattered around. My footsteps made a nice thud in the cold, motionless air, which filled my nose and lungs and made me feel sharp and alive.

I looked around and found some colors hiding in the browns and grays. Dark green pines and spruces. A red awning. A blue garage door. Red berries on a bush. The purple-black bricks of the Baxters' house. I myself was an emissary of color, moving through the world in a fluorescent red coat Chrisanne didn't know I was wearing and my eight-foot-long scarf. I trod once more over a much-trodden dirt path frozen hard as a rock, through a small bunch of trees to the Boney Dump, a flat place where the power company dumps ash and kids ride their bikes on it. As I came out into the open, snow started to fall. I sat down on a rock and watched. The snow wasn't sticking to the ground yet, but I could look at the snowflakes on my coat sleeve. I knew each one was supposed to be completely different from every other one, but I couldn't see the differences that clearly. I could see that each one had exactly six sides, which seemed amazing enough for something just falling out of the sky. An extra detail, more than anyone would expect.

The snow fell more thickly. The hills, then the houses at the far edge of the Boney Dump, disappeared behind curtains of falling flakes. It felt private, like a room, with walls you could walk through. And then someone did. Up out of the woods, just twenty feet away. I caught my breath for a second, and all the old warnings about the hoboes who were supposed to be loitering dangerously around the railroad tracks jumped into my mind. I had never actually seen a hobo. And I didn't see one now either. I saw Mr. Schimpf, of all people, huffing up out of the woods, in boots and floppy overcoat and hat with earflaps down and red nose and steamy clouds of breath. He must have walked four miles from their house in Birdvale to get there.

"Mr. Schimpf!" I said to him. "Why aren't you in church?"

"I am in church," he said.

"Me, too," said I.

He hiked on, vanishing behind the walls of snow. I wondered what had possessed him to walk so far on such a cold morning, but then look at me: I was sitting on a rock, getting accumulated on.

I sat there a little longer. The ground was white now; everything was white. There *was* something churchy about it. Everyday cares and troubles floated out of me, just far enough away so they looked interesting and manageable, none of them hopeless. Then they floated completely out of sight. Maybe I was just going into a state of bliss before freezing to death. But no, this was a peaceful, holy moment, a peaceful, holy place. I sat there a few minutes more; then I went back home.

By early afternoon the sun came out; everything was frosted and glittering. It reminded me of a department store window display of snow because it was so fresh and clean and perfect. I guess it's supposed to be the other way around, the window reminding you of the real thing. But the real thing doesn't usually stay perfect for as long. At least not in Seldem. Maybe nowhere.

CHAPTER FOURTEEN

Christmas Eve

Fʀᴀɴ ʜᴀᴅ Christmas Eve again this year. Last year she skipped it because it is such a ton of work. So we were all thrilled when she turned from her spaghetti sauce one day and said, "I'm thinking I'll have Christmas Eve, Helen. Can you come?"

My mother wrapped both hands around her coffee cup and studied an invisible calendar in space.

"Well," she said, "we're not going anywhere, but my mother will be here."

"Your mother will come, too, of course," said Fran. "You can bring a ham. And cookies. I'll need your oven."

"And card tables," said my mom. "You'll probably want both of ours."

"Do you still have those folding chairs from your church?" asked Fran.

Chrisanne and Tesey and I passed smiles across our soup; once they got this far, there was no turning back.

A notepad and pen materialized in my mother's hands, and she and Fran started going over all the details.

There were a lot of details. A lot of them had to do with fish. Italian Christmas Eve dinner is *about* fish. Unlimited fish. Soft, fat potato doughnuts stuffed with anchovies,

called cullurelli. Baccalà, which is dried cod that has to be soaked in water for a week, and the water changed every day. And calamari. This is like lasagna, and Fran made me taste it the first time and say how good it was before she told me that the noodles were pieces of squid. More squid and more baccalà get tossed with spaghetti. And there is fresh cod, and smelts.

Then, because some people don't like fish, there is regular lasagna and spaghetti, ham and a stuffed turkey. Salad, vegetables, garlic bread, little crystal dishes with olives and pickles. Mountains of fruit and nuts. Everyone brings some dish prepared with patience and great care. We all clatter down into Fran and Danny's basement and sit at tables connected by overlapping tablecloths into a long, uneven line, squeezed in between the storage area on one side and the freezer, washer, and dryer on the other side, and we eat.

The food has a magical effect of making us feel we must be the most fortunate human beings living on the earth, because what it really is, is love, disguised as food. It holds all the love we didn't find words for this year. Or maybe food is just a better way to express it.

Anyway, the words are busy doing other things. Fran is telling everybody what and how much to eat (more, of everything). Her brothers are having big arguments about which turnpike exit has a Sunoco station or which moment of which day of which year the helicopter landed in the field behind Grandma Spina's backyard.

Here's how many conversations each person is having:

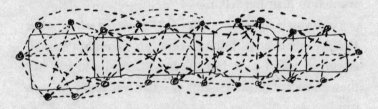

Weddings, hairdos, illnesses, new babies, new storm doors, new cars, car trouble, bad weather, bad luck, good luck, work, school, vacations, movies, TV.

Danny makes sure each glass is full of wine or pop.

After dinner, little glasses of Galliano are poured for the adults from a tall, skinny bottle. It's a sticky yellow drink that tastes like licorice. This year Chrisanne got her own glass. Tesey got one, too. I got a sip, which was all I wanted, really. It's interesting, but I'd rather eat the cookies. You wouldn't think I'd have room, but I did, at least for nibbling. Biscotti, jumbrelli, ingenetti, and thumbprints. (Guess which kind we brought, being only honorary Italians.)

Candlelight, full stomachs, and sips of Galliano warmed and melted the tangle of noisy talk down into one conversation that stretched from end to end. It thickened into the middle as people moved into seats left empty by Tesey, Chrisanne, and the cousins, who drifted upstairs to play cards and wash dishes. I was going to go, too, but Fran was telling about the plastic tomatoes my dad tied to her tomato plants and about how she changed the labels on our cans while we were on vacation, and I wanted to hear her tell it.

"Can you believe it?" she said. "I'm such a wimp. After Helen came over with the second can, I couldn't stand it anymore, and I gave her the list. I actually kept a list, that's how compulsive I am, of what was really in each can."

"She handed me this list," said my mother, laughing, with tears spilling from the corners of her eyes. "And I just looked at it. I thought, How does she know what's in my cans? It took me five minutes, even after she explained to me how she cut the labels off the cans with a razor blade and glued them on different cans—"

"You didn't think I could think of something like that, did you, Helen?"

"I couldn't believe *any*body would think of something like that."

"I *had* to tell her. She was ready to take the cans back to the A and P. I was afraid Joe down there would have a stroke; it would overload his brain, trying to figure out what happened. And then it would be my fault!"

"Hey, Fran," said Aunt Angie. "Speaking of strokes. Did you know that Vincent Peretti is in the hospital? I was at the desk when they brought him in. He had a stroke. A mild one, though. He's doing good. You should stop in and see him."

"No kidding," Fran said. "When did that happen?"

"Thursday night," said Aunt Angie. "Uncle Vincent. I was married to Tony five years before I realized he wasn't his real uncle."

Uncle Tony laughed. "You were married to me five years before *I* realized he wasn't my real uncle."

Grandma Spina smiled. "That's because he practically grew up in our house, with our family. His dad was no good. A bum. Always drinking. Vincent was afraid of him." She shook her head. "I never understood how such a kind boy come from such a mean father. Well, his mother was a nice woman, poor thing. I guess that's how."

My dad and Mrs. Tovelli blew puffs of smoke from their cigarettes and tapped them into an ashtray at just the same time, in twin movements. Mr. Tovelli's cigar added smoke to the cloud that formed there, then thinned to a haze. Grandpa Gliamocco spoke to Grandma Gliamocco in Italian, and she spoke back to him. He translated.

"Tilda says her father used to say, 'Joe Peretti wasn't mean when he wasn't drinking. The trouble was, he was always drinking.' " He looked around the table. "What do you do with someone like that?"

In the quiet of Fran and Danny's basement, there was only the muffled blur of laughter and shouting from upstairs. Here below there were a few murmurs of bafflement. No one seemed to know. Who could even think about it after all that good food?

"I was like that." It was Mr. Tovelli.

Fran said, "Oh, Frank, you were never like that."

"Sure I was," said Mr. Tovelli. "When I got back from the war. For about six months. If it wasn't for the guy I was working for, I'd be dead. He dragged me out of the bar one day and said to me, 'Frank, I'm watching you kill yourself. And not only am I watching you, my money is buying the weapon. I don't spend my money like that.' He took me to his house. He said, 'You're living here for a while.' Every day after work I went home with him. His wife fed me. I played with his kids. I slept on their couch. For three months. Then I met Joanie, and things started to make a little more sense, it got easier. I can never forget what he did for me, though."

It got quiet again then, the kind of quiet where people are wondering, What do we say now?

Finally, Uncle Tony said, "What made you drink like that, Frank?"

Mr. Tovelli shrugged his bulky shoulders. "Oh, you

know. It was the war. The war was not glamorous for me, where I was. It was not exciting. It was pretty lousy, where I was. I couldn't get it out of my head; it made me a little crazy, I guess."

"That wasn't Joe Peretti's problem," said Grandma Spina.

"Maybe not," said Mr. Tovelli. "Maybe nobody ever asked him. Did anybody ever ask him? That's all I'm saying."

My dad spoke. "My mother nearly always had someone sleeping on our couch. Half the time we didn't even look to see who it was."

"Really, Ed?" said Fran. "Like what kind of people?"

"Oh, I don't know. . . . I do remember one girl, Lila something. She got in trouble, and her mother kicked her out of the house. She was with us for a long time. She had her baby in our living room, and I think the baby was walking before she moved out."

Aunt Mary said, "People don't do that anymore, do they? People don't look out for each other the way they used to."

"Sure, they do. We just don't sleep in each other's houses anymore." Fran laughed. "We have these dumb little houses." She paused. "It does seem different, though, doesn't it?"

"It's no different," said Mr. Tovelli. "It just seems different because when we were kids, everything our parents did, we thought that was the normal thing to do.

Now we have to think about it. Just like they did. You think my boss didn't think twice before bringing a drunk home to live with his family, with his children? You think that was an everyday event for him?"

Aunt Mary said, "He knew you were a good person, Frank."

"He didn't know that," said Mr. Tovelli. "Nobody knows that."

"Now that's something I don't think I could do," said my mother.

"But you washed Bobby's clothes and made him lunch," I said.

Everyone turned and looked at me. They had forgotten I was still there.

"Whose clothes did you wash, Helen?" asked Aunt Angie.

"What are you doing here?" Fran said. "You're supposed to be upstairs washing dishes. Here. Take these glasses up, and ask Tesey if the coffee's ready."

I clinked up the metal treads of the basement stairs. As I reached the landing, I could hear my mother saying, "I just feel for the kids. It's not their fault." I carried the glasses to the sink; then I went back and sat quietly on the landing to listen some more.

After a while it was time to go home and to bed.

Chrisanne fell asleep right away, but I lay awake, looking up at the landscape on the ceiling. It was just the shadow of the curtains made by light from the electric

picture it brown and golden

Christmas candles on the windowsill, but it always looks to me like hills and trees next to a river at sunset, golden and brown like an old painting. Peaceful.

I thought about Mr. Tovelli's story and the other stories. What was the difference between Mr. Tovelli and Mr. Prbyczka, between Lila something and Marie? Okay, so maybe Mr. Prbyczka was a jerk. But maybe he wasn't. It seemed to me that the difference was that someone had cared about Mr. Tovelli, about Lila. Like the hero in a fairy tale who says to the monster, "I can see your true heart!" and then the monster turns back into some good person who was just under a spell.

But how could you know who was a good person, just under a spell?

"No one can know that," Mr. Tovelli had said. "Maybe nobody ever asked him."

"He was no good, a bum."

"Did anyone ever ask him?"

I wondered what would happen to Marie, whether I would ever see her again. And Bobby. It seemed to me that the hero was often someone outside the monster/good person's immediate family. And that maybe family boundaries are made-up lines, like state borders. And that we all need to take care of one another, somehow.

One big safety net. I tried to picture a safety net that you could help hold and be caught by at the same time. Then I decided it would be a bunch of different safety nets, maybe arranged in a circle so there would always be one underneath you. In my mind, this looked like a drawing by Dr. Seuss, and it wouldn't actually work unless the laws of gravity were changed. So maybe a safety net wasn't the best way to think about this idea. Then I thought about how the kind act can be big and dramatic or so small that only one person notices, like a smile at a hard moment. A bowl of berries.

Before I fell asleep, my mind wandered a little way into the future. It was unclear what I was doing exactly, but I was dressed like Miss Epler and I was Making My Own Life Happen. I tried to see what that meant, but besides dressing in an interesting way, it mostly seemed to mean eating pie. Oh, well, it's a start.

Patty called this afternoon, before we went to Fran and Danny's. Just to talk. She does that. It's only one of the things I really like about her. I call her, too. She comes here, I go there. I have a friend again.

I have friends.